A MAN OF THE LAW

The long-haired cowpoke faced Spur squarely. "You wouldn't be one of those homesteaders, would you?"

"No, I'm no farmer, but I'm not a rancher either. Fact is, I'm a lawyer," said Spur.

"You don't look like no lawyer to me," said a Spanish-accented voice.

"Why the hell don't you go back where you came from?" said a white-haired old hand.

Spur felt the tension increase. The men were outraged, scared. If he said the wrong thing, he could set them off like firecrackers. . . .

Also in the Spur Series:

SPUR #11

NEBRASKA NYMPH

DIRK FLETCHER

LEISURE BOOKS   NEW YORK CITY

A LEISURE BOOK®

April 2004

Published by

Dorchester Publishing Co., Inc.
200 Madison Avenue
New York, NY 10016

ISBN 0-8439-2260-5

Visit us on the web at www.dorchesterpub.com.

SPUR #11

NEBRASKA NYMPH

CHAPTER ONE

Kearney County, Nebraska
April 1874

AL PARKER wiped early morning sweat from his sunburned brow as he filled the last bucket at the outside water pump. The air hung crisply over his farm with the first hints of summer as the sun's rays slowly stretched over the flat land. Parker hefted the bucket, cursing softly as the water slopped over the side and spilled onto his trouser leg.

Then he heard it.

Riders approaching—two, perhaps three. From the west. Not many men riding this time of day, Parker thought, resting the bucket on his spattered leg and squinting into the darkness. A gray trail of dust rose along the track that led to the Parker farm.

The hair on the back of his neck rose. Parker felt the old queasiness boil up in his gut. The threats—the angry looks from the ranchers in town. Could they be riding against—

"Al! Al! Hurry up with the water!"

"Get on inside!" Al screamed, letting the bucket crash into the dirt as he turned and ran toward the farmhouse. His wife, Gilly, darkly pretty, stood in shock in the doorway.

"What's the matter, Al?"

Parker raced past her, gripped her arm and pulled her into the farmhouse with controlled strength. He grabbed the Winchester off the rack by the fireplace, filled his pockets with extra rounds, slammed the door shut and bolted it, then knelt before the parlor window facing the trail.

"Git down, Gilly," he said. "We have company. Could be them ranchers who were threatening me in town the other day."

Gilly's face, not yet worn by the strains of farm life, clouded with confusion.

"What? Whatever are you talking about? What threats?"

Parker grimaced. He had avoided telling Gilly, didn't want to upset her. They'd just moved into their new farm six months ago and things had been tough.

"Never mind. Just get Kris and go on into the kitchen. Stay clear of windows. Find a spot on the floor and don't budge. I pray to God that I'm wrong, but—"

"Al!" Gilly's hand touched his shoulder. "You're shaking!"

Parker gathered his strength and willed his body to remain still. He wasn't scared—even though that's what everybody said back in Atlanta—he was just angry. "Get Kris and do what I say!"

"All right, if you think so—"

"Do it!" he roared, so loudly that Gilly backed away from him and ran into the kitchen were their two year old daughter tearfully awaited breakfast.

Parker's glance flew from one side of the view the window afforded him to the other, scanning the entire terrain. The dust trail had dispersed, melding into the deepening gold of the morning. The riders must have dismounted, turned off the trail, or—

A window shattered, sending deadly shards of glass through the air. Gilly's scream echoed through the house.

"Gilly!"

"I'm fine, and so's Kris." Her voice was taut with fear.

"Stay put!" Parker ran to the opposite window to get a better view. Still no sign of the men—they must have dismounted and walked in. Parker saw a hint of movement out of the corner of his eye—he smashed the window with his rifle butt and planted two rounds into a newly-built shed, the rifle's recoil nearly knocking him backward. Parker had used it once or twice before. He'd always told himself he had to learn how to shoot. He hated firearms.

Sharp, stinging reports of rifles slashed through the air from three directions simultaneously. Fear mounting within him, Parker ran from window to window, from the parlor to the

7

bedroom, as rounds slammed into the house. He peeled off random shots and was reloading as another window shattered somewhere in the house. Gilly's screams punctuated each new blast.

I should have told her, Parker thought. His hands shook and he spilled a cartridge to the floor. He cursed and finished reloading, then blasted as much lead as possible at the unseen gunmen, hoping to God he'd get lucky and hit at least one of them. He didn't care about himself —it was Gilly and his sweet Kris he was protecting. He'd been an idiot to leave the comfort and safety of Atlanta to drag his family into this.

Lead shot past him and slammed into the split pine wall behind. Blinded with anger and fear, Parker's untrained hands fired round after round, the fury at the unjust attack building up within him. After a moment, all was silent. He poked his head up and peered out the window. Still no one in sight, but the air was filled with smoke.

"Hey, you in the house!" a gruff voice called. "Parker. Come on out. We don't want to hurt you. We're just having a little fun. Ain't we, boys?"

A few laughs rang out. Parker, taken completely by surprise by this new approach, didn't budge. He tried to determine the men's positions by their voices, but it was no good. He didn't know where they were holed up.

"Hey Parker, we just want to talk to you. What's the matter, afraid, little man?"

"I ain't that stupid," Parker called, then ducked and moved to a new position at another window. He didn't want his voice to give away his exact whereabouts. Being inside the house was an advantage, he thought with grim satisfaction.

"Hell, you were stupid enough to try your luck at farming. This is the worst goddamn'dest excuse for farm I ever did see."

"Leave us alone!" Gilly's voice shouted from the kitchen. "We never hurt you!"

"We will. As soon as we've got your word that you'll pack up and move out of Kearney County forever—go back to Atlanta or Augusta or wherever the hell you're from. We don't want your kind. There's no room for homesteaders in the Platte River Valley."

"We've got every right—who the hell put you in charge?" Parker screamed. "Get the hell off my property or I'll—"

"You'll what?" the gruff voice said. "We hold all the aces, Parker. Get you, your ugly brat and fat-assed woman onto the next train heading East or we'll blow you all to bits."

Parker crawled to the kitchen, where he found Gilly huddled in a corner, protecting a fidgeting Kris with her body. She started at the sound of his hands and knees shuffling across the floor, then relaxed when she saw his face.

"Al, I—" she began.

He shook his head. Gilly nodded, then stroked Kris' hair.

"We have to leave," Gilly whispered.

"No."

"You don't care what happens to us?"

Parker's face was set.

"Is that it?" Gilly asked, her voice rising. "Or is it what your friends'll say back in Atlanta?"

He looked up at her sharply.

"Please, Al. Think of me and Kris."

Parker shut his eyes tightly.

"You still in there? Come on out where we can see you, or we'll blast you all to kingdom come. That way, even though we won't be rid of you, at least you won't be fencing up prime grazing land. Course, they'll need to dig three more graves on boot hill."

"We're staying!" Parker yelled out the kitchen window, rage mounting slowly inside him. He looked back to Gilly. Her face fell; she turned from her husband and cradled Kris in her arms, as tears silently splashed down her cheeks.

Parker's news was greeted with several rounds that shook the house with their fury.

"You didn't hear me, Parker," the gruff man said, when the firing quieted. "You ain't got no choice. Go homestead somewhere else, if you're bound and determined to be a piss-poor farmer, but not here. Come on out of there or we'll come in shooting."

Parker glanced again at Gilly, but she wouldn't look at him. He snaked along the floor to the parlor and poked his head above the windowsill. If he left the farmhouse they'd probably kill him, but they might leave Gilly and Kris alone. Parker rose to his feet, beating down the vomit that churned in his stomach.

"Don't shoot!" he called as he gripped the door handle. "I'm coming out!"

"Al! Don't!" Gilly screamed from the kitchen.

"Stay put, woman!" he said, then opened the door. Slowly, his rifle in hand, Al Parker stepped into the full sunshine.

"Throw down your weapon," a man to his right said.

Parker laid it on the porch, then kicked it away.

"Why me?" he asked, his voice trembling. "I'm not the only homesteader in the county. There are plenty more, the Craigs, the—"

"You're the newest one," the únseen man said in his gruff voice.

"But—but why can't you—"

"Shut up, you blubbering asshole! If you wanna live in Kearney, be prepared to die for the honor. You got that straight?"

Parker's fears ate away at his determination. His farm, the work he'd done so far, meant nothing. All that mattered was getting Gilly and Kris safely out of Kearney. "All right. I got it straight. Look, can't we talk about this man to man? Why don't you show yourselves? I thought only cowards hid in shadows?"

A grumble emitted from his right. Parker was sure one of the men—the one doing the talking—was crouched behind a stack of old lumber near the barn.

Three men rose from their hiding places—

evenly spaced around the farmhouse. He had to crane his neck to see the third. All wore nondescript clothing and had kerchiefs hiding their lower faces.

"Here we are. Nobody calls me a coward," the gruff-voiced man said. "Especially not an asshole farmer. Why don't you get your wife to come on out too? I could use a good fuck right now." The man lewdly grabbed his crotch and laughed.

Parker's face flared with color. The man had gone too far. To his amazement he found courage. Without thinking out his actions he ducked, rolled across the porch, and had the Winchester in his hands before any of the men could stop him. As he took aim on the leader he felt a sharp, searing pain tear through his left shoulder. He screamed and dropped the rifle to the floor, where it discharged crazily into the farmhouse wall.

"Asshole!" the leader shouted. All three men had ducked back under cover.

Parker pulled himself in through the door and slammed it shut with his foot as the air filled with the sharp, acrid stench of gunpowder and piercing blasts from discharging rifles. Gilly cried out from the kitchen as Parker scrambled to his feet, the pain pounding in his shoulder. He ignored it and returned fire, moving from one window to the next, aiming for the spots the men had last hidden themselves in.

He heard a crash and twisted his head back in time to see a flaming torch fly through the air and land on their bed. The quilts and blankets instantly caught fire.

"Get the water buckets!" Parker called to Gilly as he ran for the bedroom. He grabbed a quilt from the rack by the door and slapped it at the base of the flames but backed away as they increased in heat and roared up toward the ceiling. The curtains had caught on fire too as the flaming torch had passed through them. Within moments Gilly appeared, bent over with the weight of two filled water buckets, but Al pushed her back from the inferno-like heat. He took the buckets and dumped their contents on the flames on the bed.

Water sizzled and evaporated. Angry red and orange flames licked up the walls as thick black smoke rose from the bed. Sputtering and coughing, Parker stepped back again. The water was no good; the fire had had too much of a start.

Wallpaper peeled and crackled as it burned; caches of pitch deep inside the wallboards exploded and sent out spurts of acrid white smoke.

"Jesus Christ!" Parker yelled.

Gilly turned away and ran into the kitchen. He met her as she turned back to him, holding a sobbing Kris. Gilly's eyes shone like those of a madwoman.

Over the increasing roar of the fire they heard occasional rounds from outside. Smoke filtered into the parlor from the bedroom, and Gilly screamed as flames broke out noisily in the kitchen. Parker ran there—another torch had been tossed into the house.

"What can we do?" Gilly asked, looking at the front door. Parker knew the men would never let him leave the house alive. He put his arms around Gilly and Kris and held them for a moment, then kissed his wife tenderly, though his body shook.

"I'm going out. If they kill me, stay in here as long as you can."

"But Al—"

He shook his head. The flames crept closer on both sides, approaching them with frightening speed. "I made a mistake. We could've left and never come back. I'm sorry, Gilly." He turned and ran for the door as the roar of the fire increased tenfold. Waves of heat radiated throughout the farmhouse. Gilly took three steps toward him, one arm cradling Kris, the other outstretched to him.

Parker opened the door. An instant later a round slammed into his chest, the hot lead piercing his heart and driving through his body to exit out his back. Parker saw blinding white light for a second, then fell lifelessly to the porch floorboards.

Inside the house, Gilly glanced out the broken windows. Were the men gone yet? Kris coughed and screamed in her arms. Gilly's eyes, blinded by tears and the smoke, couldn't properly focus. She finally saw the prostrate form of her husband lying on the porch, a dark red stain over his left breast.

"No!" she screamed harshly, startling the

14

child in her arms. Tears streaming down her cheeks, Gilly started for the door. Timbers crackled and twisted above her. She looked up in time to see the roof fall toward her as it burst into flames, crushing and burning them before Gilly could open her mouth to scream again.

CHAPTER TWO

THE HOMESTEAD Act passed by the United States Congress on May 20, 1862 spelled the end of the open prairies west of the Mississippi. This act provided the head of a family or an individual over the age of 21 with up to 160 acres of land, free of charge. The family simply had to take up residence on the property, cultivate and improve it for three years, and then the land was legally theirs.

Before this act huge tracts of land belonging to the U.S. government were bought and sold, sometimes at enormous profits. In 1852 the *Free Soil Democracy* stated, "That the public lands of the United States belong to the people, and should not be sold to individuals nor granted to corporations, but should be held as a sacred trust for the benefit of the people, and should be granted in limited quantities, free of cost, to landless settlers."

The debate raged politically for ten years,

with two homesteading bills drafted: one failed to pass, the other was vetoed by President Buchanan. Finally the Homestead Act of 1862 was passed. This opened up the West for countless settlers. Many of those who came were poor, homeless or adventure-seeking. Many more returned home, driven back by the hostility of the land, their own ineptitude at farming, droughts, and insect plagues. Those who stayed tamed the land and parcelled up the once free prairies, often infuriating ranchers who ran their cattle over the formerly open range. The widespread use of the newly invented barbed wire sparked outcries from ranchers, but the farmers had to protect their crops. Hostilities often grew violent. In Kearney, Nebraska, in 1874, things got downright deadly.

General Halleck was a cold, unfeeling man, Spur McCoy thought as the train screeched to a stop before a freshly-painted sign bearing the words KEARNEY, NEBRASKA. Spur hadn't more than a day off work in the last six months, and he'd already received his new assignment. Still, Spur realized that Halleck used him so much because he was the only United States Secret Service agent west of the Mississippi. Hell, he hadn't seen his office in St. Louis for months.

Spur retrieved his carpet bag, rested his favorite Spencer over his shoulder and walked off the train to the small Kearney station platform. At 6'2" and 200 pounds, well tanned, with green eyes, reddish-brown hair and a full moustache set off by sandy mutton chop side-burns, Spur was a man everyone noticed. Especially the ladies. They never seemed to mind when he spent an afternoon or evening with them.

At thirty-two he was one of a handful of Secret Service agents in the country. An excellent horseman, crack shot with most any gun, and skilled in hand-to-hand combat, knife and stick fighting, Spur McCoy was a man able to take care of himself.

Spur watched a smartly dressed woman with an ample bosom wait patiently for the passengers to leave the train, then pertly step into the passenger car where she was lost from Spur's view. Not bad for a first glimpse of a new town.

Spur turned and walked through the station and down the main street, a broad expanse of dust and mud with six blocks of unimpressive false-front buildings on both sides. The railroad had come to Kearney to ship beef to St. Louis, and Kearney had grown. Since 1862 home-steaders had been moving into the area, in turn producing more business all around. Kearney in 1874 was a bustling small prairie town, growing bigger each year.

On the surface, it wasn't an exceptional place. Spur had seen many similar towns—so many he couldn't possibly name them all. But General Halleck had warned him that the town wasn't as peaceful as it appeared to be. Two weeks ago a farmer, his wife and two year old daughter were burned to death at their farm outside

Kearney. There were also conflicting reports that the farmer, one Al Parker, had taken a slug through the heart, but the bodies were so badly burned it was impossible to be certain.

Word around town had it that the deaths were not accidental, and were a warning to the other homesteaders in Kearney County: *Move or we'll burn you out*. The ranchers were furious over the homesteaders' lavish use of the newly introduced barbed wire. The farmers were trying to save their crops from the stampeding feet of cattle, but the ranchers were used to running their cattle wherever they damned well pleased and the barbed wire was ending that.

This situation was becoming more common throughout the West, but in Kearney some ranchers evidently decided to relieve their frustrations with violence, Spur had been told. If it had been an innocent homestead family murdered by ranchers, it was Spur's job to discover the murderers and hand them over to the proper authorities. He also needed to diffuse the tension between rancher and farmer in the Platte River Valley.

Spur checked in at the Calico Hotel, dropped his bag and rifle in his room, then headed for the nearest saloon. It was Peterson's, the only one in town, a two story building with a fancy sign.

McCoy pushed through the bat-wing doors into the fairly clean, smoke-filled saloon.

"Hold it right there, asshole!" a man's high-pitched voice said.

Spur's hand automatically flew to the holster he had tied down on his right leg, but quickly realized the words weren't directed at him.

"Fuck you," another man said, snarling as he leaned against the bar. He was twenty-five, with an angry expression fired with whiskey. His clothes indicated his occupation: farming. Blond hair spilled around his weathered face. Spur noticed that although the man appeared to be relaxed, his hands hung loose but ready for instant action.

The other man stood across the saloon, in shadows. Spur could faintly make out his outline, and the glint of steel where a kerosene's light penetrated that far.

"Damned sodbuster! Take back what you said!" The voice was turgid with emotion.

"I don't know what you're talking about." The farmer's words were smooth and easy. He drained his whiskey glass, set it back on the bar, and motioned for another.

Spur gauged the reactions of the few men scattered around the bar, and was surprised to see a pretty woman in a red, frilly dress that matched her red hair sitting at a table near the center of the bar, apparently unafraid.

"I heard what you said about ranchers—god-damn it!" the man in the shadows said. "Look at me! Turn around and face me like a man!"

Having received his drink, the farmer downed it, threw the glass to the floor, and spun around. In a smooth, easy style Spur greatly admired, his hand slipped to his right, gripped the pearl handle of the Colt Peacemaker, and swung it up, perfectly aimed at the man. He could have blasted the rancher into the next world in a split second. Instead, he grinned insolently.

"I don't give a fuck what you think," the farmer said slowly, enunciating each word carefully.

As he watched the scene play itself out, he realized the man wasn't drunk. This confrontation confirmed Halleck's message—there was tension between the farmers and ranchers. He'd walked in on a fine example.

The shadowed figure took three steps forward. The man was dressed in ranching work clothes, his jaw freshly shaven, black hair perfectly parted in the middle framing his anger-marred fleshy face. A fattened rancher, Spur decided immediately. His hand hovered over the handle of his Colt .44.

To Spur's surprise, the red-dressed woman rose to her feet, standing almost between the men.

"Put your guns away, boys. The boss doesn't like blood messing up his floor." The woman turned her tightly-packed body to each in turn, smiling.

"Git out of the way, Roxanna," the rancher said. "I'm gonna blow that damned farmer to hell."

"The hell you are, Fred! The only blowing that'll be done around here I'll do, thank you!"

The saloon rocked with laughter.

"Relax, Roxanna," the farmer said smoothly. "You know better than anyone in town that ranchers got no dicks."

"Goddamn you!" the rancher said, and started to draw his iron.

The woman rushed him, then kicked the gun from the rancher's hand. It rattled to the floor.

"Leave me alone, Roxanna!" the rancher said as he grabbed her wrists. She fought back, laughing, and finally wrestled her way free of him.

Roxanna pushed back a wisp of hair that had fallen from her head and planted her hands on her hips. "Go on back home, Fred. No sense in getting thrown in jail for nothing. Go on!"

"No woman tells me what to do," Fred said menacingly.

This set up another round of guffaws from the men in the saloon. Spur glanced back at the blond farmer. He just caught the man holstering his weapon and walking out of the saloon.

"Showed up by a woman!" one man said, slapping another's back.

The rancher walked past Roxanna and stomped out the door after the farmer. With the excitement finished, the men went back to shuffling cards, drinking, and smoking. Roxanna laughed again as if the incident had been a joke and sat at a table.

Spur bought a whiskey and stood next to the bar. He downed the shotglass of booze in one gulp and the bartender wordlessly replaced it. McCoy sipped his second drink as the man next to him turned and stared at Spur.

"I don't recognize you," the man said after a few moments. Light brown stubble covered his cheeks and spilled down on either side of his thin face. A pinkish-red scar snaked along his right cheek. He stood about two inches shorter than Spur's six feet two, slightly leaner as well. What held Spur most about the man's face were the blue eyes. They seemed infused with deep, violent emotion.

"I'm new in town," Spur said, after summing up the man as he'd been analyzed.

"That wasn't a smart thing to do," he said. "Roxanna breaking up that fight. She should have let them have it out. I'd have liked to seen that farmer blast that rancher into hell."

"Why?" Spur asked.

"Because he's a rancher. That's good enough reason for me. If only Roxanna had—" He trailed off.

Spur sipping the biting, warm liquid. "You a farmer?" He damned well knew the answer.

"Yeah. Carl Lanford."

"Spur McCoy. I take it this isn't the first confrontation between farmers and ranchers here?"

"Shit no! It's been going on for years—but now with barbed wire we can fence those bastards off our land. Now the ranchers are really getting mad, cause we can fight back. At first they just stampeded across our fields, knocked over our buildings, that kind of thing. But two weeks ago the Parkers were murdered. Ranchers have gone just about as far as they can."

"You think some ranchers killed these Parkers?"

"Damn straight. Hell, I don't like to come into

town. I hate it here. I come in twice a week, maybe once a week, to buy supplies for my farm. Too many ranchers flaunting their money and power here to suit my tastes. But of course, there's other reasons for coming to Kearney—like that red-headed bitch that broke up the fight."

Spur glanced over at Roxanna, who sat entertaining a young man at his table.

"I see what you mean," Spur said conversationally. At least it wasn't difficult to get people to talk. Lanford might know plenty. "Someone got killed?"

"Yeah. The Parkers. Al and Gilly and their kid. Christ, they were good people. Hard working, from Atlanta. Just trying to make a go at farming, though they never really fit in well around here. They moved to Kearney County about half a year ago, homesteading. Now they're dead—and those damned ranchers killed them!"

"You know that for sure?"

"You're goddamned right I know for sure! Christ, word got around town real quick. Some think the men went there to scare the Parkers away, but that something went wrong and they killed them. I don't think so. Those ranchers went out there to kill the Parkers as a warning. Can't be any other way."

"I see. Any idea who did it?"

Lanford snorted. "If I did they wouldn't still be breathing. I got my suspicions, but nothing for certain." Lanford glanced up at Spur. "You seem mighty interested in all this, McCoy."

Spur shrugged. "Just making conversation."

The men were silent for a few moments, and Spur collected his thoughts. Things were heating up in Kearney. He'd come at the right time, before the whole country erupted into a farmer-rancher war with heavy losses on both sides.

Spur understood the problem from both viewpoints. Unfortunately, the ranchers and farmers couldn't do that. The hardest thing to accept, Spur thought, is change. The West was changing and the men who lived there had to as well.

"Who were those two men just now?" Spur asked.

Lanford started somewhat—then recovered and downed the rest of the drink. "The ranchers are getting more ornery, more sure of themselves," he said, ignoring Spur's question. "I hate all ranchers—I'd kill them all if I could. Especially that one," he said, motioning to the door through which the rancher had recently departed. "Things like this happen all the time —in the saloon, on the street, even in the general store. Hell, I heard about Roxanna going at it hot and heavy with some cowboy, only to have a rancher pull him off her to go at it. The rancher got his pants down before the farmer got back on his feet and the two men set to fisting it out. It ended with the rancher chasing the farmer butt-naked out into the street." Lanford's face grew dark. "But now it's gone beyond that. They're ruling this area, squeezing the life out of us."

"Think the farmers will retaliate for the Parker killings?"

"Hell, I don't know. Maybe. I wouldn't put it past some of the men I know. They're not only scared, they're damn mad. If the ranchers killed the Parkers, who's next? That's on my mind every night when I go to sleep. I go to bed with a loaded rifle." The man's face suddenly looked haggard, and Spur wondered how much sleep the man actually enjoyed. "Shit, I should be moving on." Lanford set the glass down and walked toward the door.

"Good talking with you," Spur said to the retreating man, then swung back to the bar.

The situation in Kearney was as volatile as the message from General Halleck had indicated. Spur had met many ranchers and they weren't ordinarily the type who would kill three innocent people in cold blood. The local sheriff, a man named Gardner, Spur remembered from the telegram, hadn't had any luck in finding the Parkers' murderers, and had called to the U.S. government for help.

Spur figured it should be fairly easy—if the killings were done by ranchers, that automatically narrowed the number of possible murderers. Certainly no farmer killed the Parkers, unless there was some sort of rivalry or fight that Lanford didn't know about. Not likely.

Spur turned his back on the bar and leaned against it. Roxanna, the fancy woman, approached him slowly, her hips swinging gently and her breasts bouncing with each step.

27

She kept her eyes down as she approached him. When she stood three feet away she halted, riveted her stare on Spur's crotch, then after a few moments looked up and smiled deliciously at him, her pink tongue visible between her lips.

"What's your name?" she asked in a high, light voice.

"Spur McCoy, ma'am." Spur tipped his Stetson to her.

"McCoy. Want to come to my room for some fun?" She moved closer until she fitted her feet between his. A warm hand traveled down between their bodies and rested on the lump between his legs, pressing and fingering. "I'm good. I'm real good."

Spur felt his body responding, but with an effort moved away from the woman.

"I just got into town. Business. I don't have the time."

She looked down at the growing bulge between his legs and laughed shortly. "*He* thinks differently," she said, extending a slender finger toward his crotch.

Spur smiled. "He doesn't think. I do."

Roxanna put her hands on her hips and sighed. "Okay. Maybe next time. How long will you be in town, Spur?"

"A week, probably; maybe longer. Depends."

"On what?"

Spur looked directly into her eyes. "On how much rest you give me."

She laughed again, a hearty, musical laugh unfettered by common standards of femininity.

"I can say this for you, Spur McCoy. I like your style. Is the rest of you as inviting?"

"I don't have many complaints," Spur said, deadpan.

Roxanna laughed again. "Next time, Spur. It's you and me." She sauntered off to another prospective customer.

Spur smiled and swung back to the bar. He lifted his glass to down its contents.

"Ranchers!" a man near him said, and followed it up by spitting on the floor.

CHAPTER THREE

WE SHOULD have waited, he thought as they continued to ride through the endless, dusty prairies that made up the vast majority of the state of Nebraska. It was too light yet. They should have waited until night, so they could cover their tracks better. The blond-haired man glanced over at his riding companion, staring straight ahead, eyes riveted on the position of the still unseen ranch that was their destination.

He was a strange one, Hiram thought, and smirked as he looked away. But he'd worked for worse, and when the man had approached him in a saloon in a town he happened to be passing through, the man's offer of pay sounded interesting. Hiram remembered how he'd been wondering how he'd pay for his next drink of whiskey.

After the stranger had set a full whiskey bottle before him at the bar and said, "Drink

31

up," he propositioned Hiram—$30 for an afternoon's work. Hiram had taken the offer—and he didn't mind if he had to kill.

But this guy was a strange man. All show and no guts, he thought. He wanted another man dead. That was common enough, but this guy seemed crazy about it. Couldn't talk or think of anything else.

His partner—Hiram didn't know his name—drew rein and motioned for him to do so as well. His eyes flickered nervously back and forth, constantly on the alert, his full attention now turned toward detecting the presence of other human beings.

No one was around. They hadn't been followed from Kearney. Hiram relaxed as they rested their horses. It was at least an hour until sunset, maybe two. They should have waited.

"I know what you're thinking," the stranger said suddenly. "I can see it on your face. We shouldn't have come out here until sundown. I know. But I need the light to look around the place. I've been out there once before, earlier today, but I've got to get the lay of the land."

"I see," Hiram said, surprised by the man's forethought. Perhaps he was more than he appeared to be.

"Let's go."

They nudged their horses into action, bolting them forward due north. Hiram looked over at his partner; the man clenched and unclenched one fist.

* * *

Spur walked into the whitewashed wooden structure that bore a carefully painted sign: SHERIFF'S OFFICE. It was dark—the building had few windows and those were small. He stepped into the office area, with desk, an impressive shelf of books. potbelly stove, and a framed oil painting of President Grant. Behind this were two cells: the local jail. Both were empty.

A man swept the corner of the jail, carefully moving piles of dust closer to each other until they merged into one large mass. He looked up as the door banged shut behind Spur. He was 50, stood 5'8", balding. The remaining hair was short-cropped and black, streaked with gray. The prominent nose poked out between two friendly, honest eyes. The man's face was fleshy, guarded.

"Sheriff?" Spur asked.

"That's right," he said, placing the broom in the corner. "Jerry Gardner."

"I'm Spur McCoy. Just got into town a few hours ago."

At the mention of the name Gardner's face suddenly grew serious. "Mr. McCoy, am I glad to see you. Have a seat." He motioned to the chair that sat before his plain wooden desk.

The two men settled down facing each other.

"I really need your help," the sheriff began. "I've—I've done my best, but there's been so much trouble I haven't been able to keep track of it. And all my ideas—they just don't add up." Gardner stared out the window, the afternoon sun hitting his face harshly, turning it into a mass of wrinkles and worry lines. "I'm not the best lawman. I'm old and tired."

Spur shook his head. "I don't think so. Tell me why you brought me here."

"Didn't your man—"

"Yes, I got General Halleck's version, but I want it from you. Don't leave out anything."

Spur listened to the sheriff's story. It matched Halleck's information.

"That's as much as I know," Gardner said. "And I couldn't do anything."

"Bullshit, Gardner," Spur said. The man felt sorry for himself, had lost his self-confidence. That could kill a man faster than a drawn revolver. "You wouldn't be behind that desk if you weren't either capable or crooked, and I don't think you're crooked."

"Thanks," Gardner said.

"Only a sheriff who cared about his town would send for help. I don't think less of you for it, and neither should you."

"Hell, McCoy, sometimes I think it's time I stepped down. I don't have what I used to."

"Why?" Spur asked. "Because you can't draw as fast as you could thirty years ago? Or because your shoulders hurt sometimes, or your brain doesn't work quite as well as it used to?" Spur smirked. "I don't want to hear any more of *your* problems, sheriff. Fill me in on *Kearney's* problems. What's happened in the last few days?"

Gardner sighed, then leaned back. "No more murders, thank God. Ahh—little things. Fences being cut. Cows moving from one herd to another overnight, or disappearing completely. Crops torn up by careless hooves. Still, it's not over yet."

"Why?"

"Folks are upset here. You can see it in their faces, read it in the way they walk down the street. They aren't friendly anymore—not until they've decided which *side* you're on." He shook his head. "We used to be neighborly. I don't like this."

"Have there been any more threats?"

"Sure," Gardner said. "All the time. They don't amount to much. But they're fuel for the fire, that's for certain."

Spur was silent for a moment. "Where should I start looking?"

Gardner sat up and fumbled through the papers on his desk. "I've got it here somewhere —damn!" The man took a pen, dipped it into the well, and scribbled on a piece of paper for a few minutes while Spur sat and watched. "I forgot to do this earlier," he said. "I knew I didn't do something."

Occasionally the sheriff would pause, place the pen's point to his tongue, blackening it slightly, then resume writing. In a few minutes Gardner handed Spur the paper.

"Here's a list of the ranchers in Kearney County that I know are more than a mite angry at the homesteaders. I'm not saying either side's right, but these men have suffered the most of the farmer's wrath."

"Why's that?"

35

"They have property near farms, or run their cattle over what used to be open range, although technically it was owned by the government. I've listed them in no real order, just as they came to mind. As you can see, I've also included little descriptions of each and directions on finding their ranches."

"Fine," Spur said. "Any suggestions on who to contact first? Who'd be the most productive for me?"

Gardner shrugged. "Don't know. Maybe the Tates, although it's only one of them that dislikes farmers—that's Roscoe Tate, as you can see."

Spur read the list over carefully. There were six names. He waited for the ink to dry before folding it and tucking it into his pocket.

"Are the ranchers organized? Do you think the attack on the Parkers was a group effort? Think they may be getting some sort of secret band together to drive the homesteaders out of Kearney?"

"Damned if I know," Gardner said defensively. "It's a possibility, and one that I've thought of before, but there's no proof."

"No one witnessed the Parker killings?"

The sheriff shook his head. "No one I can find."

"And no one saw anyone ride toward the farm that morning, or away from it?"

"Damnit, Spur, I've already gone over those questions a thousand times in my mind. No one saw anything—or if they did, they aren't talking."

"Sorry, Gardner. I have to ask."

He lifted a hand and waved it in the air as if to dispel the tension. "I know. I'm sorry I yelled. This thing's been pressing on me for two weeks now. The whole town's in an uproar about it, and even some of the ranchers are angry, probably because they think they'll be blamed for the murders. In a way, they're all responsible."'

Spur rose. "Thanks for the information, Gardner. I'm sure I'll find those killers."

Gardner rose and extended his hand. "It's great to have you here, Spur. God knows I can use your help."

They shook hands and Spur headed out into the dusty street.

Sunset. The two men stood and stretched their aching limbs amidst the shelter of a willow thicket. They were on the grounds of the Lucas ranch, a mile from the farmhouse. As the sun set a cool breeze blew up for a few brief seconds, stirring the trees around them into noisy action, then quieting as the wind died. A full moon hung in the eastern sky.

"Now?" Hiram asked, looking at his boss. He was eager to get this over with. Hiram wanted his pay and a good meal in his stomach within three hours.

"Soon."

Hiram turned away from the man then, to hide his look of disgust. The man was losing his courage. He'd waited too long; the anger or fear or bitterness had passed and it was too late.

"I've thought it over. We'll wait, get him while he sleeps."

"Sleeps?" Hiram asked incredulously.

"Right. We wait six hours."

Hiram had turned half-dumb by the time the luminescent moon had climbed directly overhead. Finally his employer gave the signal and they mounted their uneasy horses. By moonlight they picked their way toward the ranchhouse, glowing white in the darkness.

"No noise," the stranger said. "We take him alone—quietly. No shooting until or unless there's no other way." He lowered his voice substantially as they neared the house. "We'll knock him out, take him outside."

"Right," Hiram said, wondering what tortures the man had in mind for his enemy.

They drew rein a quarter mile away in another clump of willows, tied up their horses, then walked silently toward the still ranchhouse.

No lights shone from the windows; the bunkhouse as they passed it was quiet. The ranch lay sleeping as they approached the house. It was a one story, unpretentious structure.

Which room was the bedroom? Hiram hoped the man knew. He sweated. This wasn't the kind of work he was used to. He liked things noisy—guns blasting, men falling to the dirt—not sneaking into houses at night.

The man walked up to the front door and turned the knob. It moved and the door swung open. Apparently the rancher wasn't expecting trouble. They walked in and turned immediately to the right, then down a hallway. At its end they came to a half-shut door. His boss pushed it open—a man lay snoring.

Motioning the other man to be quiet, they walked to the bed. Hiram's employer hefted his rifle and struck the man sharply on the head. He grunted and lay still, his breathing at a much reduced rate. He was unconscious.

They carried the man's limp body from his bed and down the hall, finally outside. As they hefted it back to their clump of willows the man flinched, rolled his head from side to side. Hiram, holding his legs, dropped them and punched the man's jaw. His head fell sideways.

Moments later Hiram stood still, holding up the man's body by the armpits while his employer pushed a noose around his neck. The other end of the rope stretched over the highest branch in a walnut tree that grew near the willow grove. Once the noose had been tightened, Hiram dropped the man to the ground.

"Roll him over."

Hiram did so and watched as the other man tied the wrists tightly together behind his back.

"Now we wake him," he said, smiling.

"Why don't we just hang him and get it over with?" Hiram asked. "What's this about waking him up?"

The other man ignored him and produced a bucket of water which he'd apparently hidden earlier. Hiram's employer threw the bucket's contents over the man's face.

He spluttered and shook his head, fighting off the sensation of drowning.

"Fred Lucas," his boss said. "You're going to die."

The man's eyes weren't open yet, and Hiram wondered if the man heard.

"You're finally getting what you've been deserving for a long time."

Lucas woke fully, blinking against the icy cold water that continued to slide down his forehead.

"Let's get him up."

Hiram rushed to the end of the rope and the two men hoisted Lucas off the ground. After securing the rope around a tree trunk Hiram's boss yanked it twice. Lucas gagged, retched, kicking the air while struggling to free his hands.

"Hold him still," the man said after standing in front of Lucas. Hiram rushed around behind him and gripped the man's legs. His employer produced a six-inch blade from a sheath that hung from his belt. It gleamed in the moonlight as he plunged it deep into Lucas' gut, grunting with the effort.

It cleaved the skin neatly. He thrashed the blade, bursting the internal organs, ripping the man's belly apart.

Lucas groaned in agony and tried to kick free of Hiram's hands. Blood spurted out, staining the ground where it dropped. He finally pulled the blade out, slimy with blood and dark tissues.

"Enough," he said, then stuffed a piece of

cloth into Lucas' mouth. "Don't want anybody to find you before you're dead."

Hiram watched the man stoically; a messy death, sure, but where's the excitement? The adventure? He sighed. At least he'd be paid.

"Let's go."

The two men made their way through the willows to the horses. No one had been alerted. Hiram pulled himself up into the saddle and frowned. It had been a good night's work. One man was happy, another dead. That's the way of life, Hiram thought as they rode quietly from the area. He drew up alongside the man. He'd been wrong about him. The guy knew what he wanted and had gotten it.

"When do I get paid?" Hiram asked.

The other man halted his horse. They were well away from the ranch.

"Now." He reached into his vest pocket.

Hiram tensed. Was this a trick? Would he pull out a revolver and blow him to hell?

No. The man produced a small bag and handed it to him. Inside he found three ten dollar gold pieces. He pocketed the money.

"Thanks."

Hiram turned away from the trail that led back to Kearney. On to the next town, the next job, and a warm woman who'd share her bed with him for a few hours.

CHAPTER FOUR

THE TATE Ranch, situated five miles outside of Kearney, was one of the largest in the area. With its four sections and 5000 head of cattle the Circle T sprawled over the flat land of the Platte River Valley and swept up into the plains.

David Tate, twenty-eight, his curly red-brown hair spilling around his handsome face, moved closer to the man lying wheezing and coughing on the bed. David's face was concerned. His father was dying, and nothing could be done about it.

Three doctors had already examined him—one brought in especially from St. Louis—but Dick Tate's disease had mystified them all. Now, six months after his father had first contracted the mysterious illness, David Tate ran the ranch, with the advice and guidance of his mother, Amanda.

As he approached his father, David choked back a grimace of pain. Dick Tate looked ancient, far older than his fifty-five years would indicate. It wasn't the harshness of ranch life, nor the power of the relentless sun that had carved the age onto the man's face—it was the strange wasting disease that sapped his strength.

"David," his father said slowly, coughing out the word.

"How you feelin', Father?" David sat on the edge of the bed and gazed down at his father. After six months it was still hard for him to see his father in this condition.

The man waved off the question. "You know how I am," he grumbled, and set into a coughing fit. When he'd quieted, Dick Tate looked up gravely at his son. "How's the ranch? Everything fine?"

David smoothed on a smile. "Yes. No problems I can think of."

"Bullshit," his father said softly. "There's always problems on the Circle T or any ranch. Don't hold back on me now, son. There's nothing I can't take."

"You always knew when I was lying, didn't you?" David asked, then brushed back salt and pepper hair from his father's head. "No real trouble. We lost twenty head—probably to rustlers. There's no sign of them anywhere."

His father frowned. "Twenty head? Shit."

"That's what I said," David said, laughing softly. "Along with that, one of the cowboys— Cole was his name, I think—came to the back door and asked to talk with mother. She refused, of course—he had no right—but he pushed past her anyway and went in. He asked her for something, and as soon as she'd left the room he rifled it of everything he could carry and then left the ranch and the county in a damn big hurry."

"What'd he take?" Dick asked huskily.

"A bag of silver dollars—"

Dick winced.

"A pair of candlesticks—oh yes, and a book. I don't remember which one."

"Not too bad."

"That's why I didn't want to disturb you. You've got to save your strength. Don't worry about the ranch—everything's fine, or will be when you're back to normal."

Dick shook his head. "I'll die in this bed, son. You know that."

David couldn't speak.

"How's Roscoe been lately? He hasn't been in to see me for two days."

The young man suddenly found words.

"Roscoe's an idiot, as you well know. He's trying to stir up trouble in town against the homesteaders."

Dick snorted. "What?"

"Yeah. I heard all about it when I rode into town this morning. Seems he wants to drive the homesteaders out of the county. I think he'll use any means."

"He didn't have nothing to do with the Parker killings, did he?"

David sighed. "Don't know. In fact, I don't

know what Roscoe's capable of doing anymore. The hot-headed ranchers are still badgering the homesteaders and I don't think it's gonna stop soon. Roscoe's in the middle of it, trying to keep the situation alive, rustling up support in the other ranchers to drive the farmers out of the county." He shook his head. "I don't like what he's doing, Father. It's not right."

"And you don't like Roscoe, do you?"

David lowered his eyes. "He's not the same since he came back. He's tougher, wilder. And I think he's jealous of my position, running the ranch."

"Can you blame him?' Dick Tate smiled. "If he hadn't run off ten years ago he'd be in your place now. Not many men can accept the consequences of their actions." Dick Tate dissolved into a coughing fit.

A moment later David turned to the second story window to see Roscoe riding toward the house.

"Here he comes," David said.

"I remember the day he left. He said he was tired of ranching and wanted to see the world. So he took that $500 from the safe—his *inheritance* he called it—and left."

"I remember too. It was my eighteenth birthday—what a shitty day to pick for doing a thing like that."

"Don't be too hard on your brother," Dick said. "He's blood. Roscoe's had a rough life, same as us. I think he's touched in the brain now, just a bit. Watch him, David. Don't be too obvious, but let me know what he's up to. God knows we certainly don't want any trouble, here on the ranch or anywhere in the county. If he is doing this—stirring up hard feelings against the farmers—I don't know what will happen. Someone's got to stop him."

"Me?"

Dick shook his head. "No. Roscoe'd never take to you giving him orders. It'll have to be Amanda or me. I don't know if we have any control over him anymore. Oh, we could kick his butt off the ranch, if it comes to that. But Roscoe seems—untameable, like that one bay I never could break."

"I know what you mean," David said, then heard the scraping of feet behind him. He turned and saw his brother standing in the doorway.

"Untameable, am I?" Roscoe asked in his guttural voice. "I take that as a compliment." The man crossed his arms over his chest and laughed heartily. "That's what Roxanna calls me."

At thirty, Roscoe Tate was in fine shape. He was 6'2", barrel chested, with powerful arms and legs honed by years of tough work. A brown moustache curled down around his mouth, and green eyes stared intently at all that came into his field of vision. His hard chin, planed jaw and hair-swept forehead all combined to make him popular with the ladies—those who charged and those who did not.

"Hello, Roscoe," Dick said. "Nice of you to stop by."

Roscoe's face didn't alter. "I've been busy, so

I haven't had time to come up here." He moved into the room and turned his attention to David. "Well, little brother, since you're running the Circle T shouldn't you be out there doing something?" He pointed toward the window.

Rage welled up inside him but David wouldn't show it in front of his father. "I'm filling Father in on the ranch. That's work, but I'm not surprised you didn't recognize it."

"Oh yeah? Sounded like you were talking about me—untameable, wasn't it? Now that doesn't sound like ranch business to me." His smile faded and his neck tightened. "That sounds like my business."

"Can it, Roscoe!" Dick Tate said, a little too forcefully, and he collapsed into a coughing fit.

"See what you've done?" David gestured toward their father. "Can't you think of anything but yourself?"

"Seems like you're doing a lot of thinking about me," Roscoe said.

"That's right. You're part of the ranch—at least, you're living here, though you're not doing an inch of work. That concerns me, as does everything connected with the Circle T."

"Look, little brother, if you were cold and dead do you know where I'd be right now?"

David stiffened visibly. He wouldn't give his brother the satisfaction of an answer.

Roscoe's green eyes shone excitedly. "If you were dead, I'd be running the Circle T." He walked two paces closer and clapped a hand down on David's shoulder. "Think about that, little brother."

David wrenched from his brother's grip and turned back to his father, who had finally ended his coughing spell and lay wheezing.

"I'll do what I can about that little matter," David said to his father, then turned to leave the room. His brother caught his arm but David pulled free. "Keep your fucking hands off me, Roscoe! I don't know who the hell you are, but you're not my brother. Not anymore."

"What a relief!" Roscoe said grimly. "To think after all these years—"

"That's enough!" Dick Tate said from his bed. Both men turned to look at him.

"Roscoe, I'll not have you treat your brother that way. Not on the Circle T!"

"Come on, Father. You know I'm just—"

"I don't give a good goddamn what you're doing! You won't do it in my presence, or in my house."

Roscoe's eyes narrowed. "Are you telling me what to do, old man?"

David spun and wildly threw a punch at his brother, which Roscoe easily deflected.

"You can't even fight like a man, baby brother. Maybe that's your trouble—you're not a man."

"Don't listen to him," Dick said to his younger son. "You remember what I said." His voice grew husky and harsh. "Now leave. I need some sleep." He pulled the quilts higher and settled back onto the goosedown pillow.

"Glad to get out of here," Roscoe said. "I'm going to get a drink. God knows I need one."

David shot past Roscoe out the door. Roscoe's

laugh echoed in the bedroom as David walked down the hall and stairs, then out the front door into the blinding Nebraska sunshine.

"Jesus Christ!" David said. Roscoe had lost all control, all feelings. Or had he? Perhaps he was just drunk. Roscoe got drunk every day, David knew. But he hadn't smelled liquor on the man's breath. Why the hell didn't his father kick Roscoe off the Circle T? Could he still feel anything for his son who treated him so cruelly? David shook his head and stared out over the vast expanse of the Tate ranch. Someday, he knew, it would be his. He didn't want it right now—God no. He didn't want his father to die. But he would get it eventually. When that day came, he'd be certain his brother never set foot on the Circle T again.

Roscoe Tate ambled down the stairs and went into the first floor study where he poured a drink of whiskey. He swallowed it straight and repeated the process. A warm glow radiated from his stomach, soothing his nerves and making him feel fine and happy.

His asshole brother David was up to something. He knew it. Roscoe could feel it in his bones. Maybe he shouldn't have said all those things in front of his father—but hell, the old man was almost dead. In a week or two—three at most—it wouldn't matter anymore. It was not that he wanted the Circle T. He'd hate to be saddled with the work, problems and headaches. Let his brother run the spread. He could loaf and drink and play with the fancy ladies in town.

Roscoe wanted the Circle T to grow richer and more prosperous year by year. Then when there was sufficient money in the bank he'd withdraw, say, ten thousand dollars and leave, never to return.

The plan had almost worked before—he'd stayed away for ten years. But his money had run out long before that; he had taken too little and spent it too fast.

Roscoe had a plan now—a better plan. With the money he'd find a good town and open a saloon. Bring in a few fancy women from St. Louis and let the cowboys and homesteaders drink and fuck their money out of their pockets and into Roscoe's.

His stupid, snivelling little brother wanted the Circle T. What an asshole! Roscoe poured another drink, then wet his mouth with the burning amber liquid, feeling it wash around with its fiery power.

He knew he'd better get rich quick or it'll be too late. Opening a saloon in a boom town farther west would do the trick, and he'd have the strongest whiskey and prettiest women anywhere around.

Roscoe shook his head. He was daydreaming again. He had to concentrate on the present, on his immediate plans. He'd heard that they'd lost twenty head, rustled from the ranch. That would cost whoever did it. He'd heard rumors around town that some farmers were killing cattle and hiding the carcasses. There was also someone else rustling in the area. These problems didn't make for good cattle business. If any upstart homesteaders were picking off cattle branded with a capital T and a circle—he wouldn't rest easy until he found who was doing it.

The thought of the homesteaders jolted a nervous twitch over his left eye into action. He hated them. Those stupid sodbusters, their weak women and scrawny babies. He wished every one of them would keel over dead or move out of the Platte River Valley. The trouble was, he also knew the homesteaders wouldn't move out by themselves. They needed help. Roscoe grinned, thinking of the kind of help he could give them.

His attention was drawn to the family Bible, with its glorious gold-stamped leather spine four inches thick. Roscoe stared at it for a moment, then smirked as he worked out his plan and poured another drink.

CHAPTER FIVE

Spur McCoy went back to his hotel, the Calico. He asked the clerk how the food was in the dining room.

"Tolerable. Just got a new cook hired on. The last one made everything taste like stewed dog. They're just putting supper down now."

Spur thanked the man and headed into the dining room. After a filling meal of a thick steak, mashed potatoes and gravy, corn and peas, topped off with coffee and apple pie with cheese, Spur went up to room 201. He had made sure he got a room situated at the end of the building, facing the street, near the outside stairs.

Spur reached out to push the skeleton key into the door's lock beneath the handle—and the door slowly swung into the room. Spur tensed and kicked the door fully open.

He heard a surprised yelp and saw a beautiful young woman sitting on his bed, her knees drawn up, the booted feet resting on the edge of the mattress. She had been playing solitaire—the cards were spread out on the quilt. When she saw Spur she lowered her feet and stood.

"Hello," she said in a high, musical voice. She looked about twenty, just under five feet even, with milky-white, smooth skin. Cascades of blonde ringlets spilled over her shoulders and back onto the skin-tight, white, high-necked bodice of her satin dress. Spur looked at her thrusting breasts. A dimpled chin and high cheekbones gave the woman a stunning face.

"Good evening, ma'am," Spur said, tipping his hat. "Mind if I ask what you're doing here?"

"Not at all, Mr. McCoy—but it's Miss."

He looked at her use of his name in surprise.

"I checked the registry," she explained. "I'm Ginny Burriss. I saw you walking into the hotel earlier, and I wanted to meet you."

Spur liked this woman, and not only physically.

"Why?"

The woman's gaze dropped to the floor. "Well, when I saw how tall and strong you are, and how handsome . . ." Her cheeks slowly flushed red. Ginny lifted her head and looked at Spur. "I just had to meet you, Mr. McCoy. You're such a man, like one I'd see in my dreams."

Spur smiled. He had heard this kind of overture from women before, and it never failed to surprise him.

"Thank you, Miss Burriss. I take that as a

compliment. You're certainly beautiful yourself."

"Really?" She looked at him in wonder.
"Maybe I am. Oh, and call me Ginny, Spur. Do
you mind if I call you that?"

"You can call me anything you want." Spur
closed the door half way for propriety, then
hung his hat on the knob and turned back to an
expectant Ginny Burriss.

"I hope this doesn't shock you, my being here
this way," she said. "But I—I just had to meet
you." She suddenly raced across the room and
flung her compact, rounded body against Spur.
Ginny clasped her arms around him and buried
her head against his powerful chest, grinding
her thighs against his.

"Not shocked at all, Ginny. As a matter of
fact, I like it."

She broke free of him. "You do?" she said,
delighted. "I'm so glad. I never have any fun—
cooped up at home all day. That's why I had to
meet you." Her eyes grew intense. "Let's
hurry." She turned her back to Spur. "Unbutton
my dress, Spur, quickly. I can't wait much
longer!"

Spur deftly freed the pearl buttons from their
satiny prisons until the back of the dress lay
open. Meanwhile, Ginny removed her boots,
pressing her firm bottom against Spur's crotch.
He pulled the bodice down and reached in to
cup her warm, firm breasts and squeeze the
nipples.

"Oh Spur, yes! Play with them! Your hand

feels so good!" Ginny sighed at his ministrations for a moment, then whirled around again. She pulled down, then stepped from the dress, which she threw into a corner.

Spur walked to the door, closed and locked it, and pushed a straight chair top under the door knob. He didn't want to be disturbed.

"You look better and better," he said, feeling warmth flow to his groin while he stared at her silk-clad body. The chemise did nothing to hide her perfectly formed breasts, the nipples already pushing out firm and erect against the smooth cloth.

"Don't just stand there, Spur," she said. "Undress me!"

McCoy slipped the chemise off her body, then bent his head to take one perfect breast in his mouth. He sucked and licked the nipple, taking it between his teeth and gently chewing.

"Oh God, Spur, yes!" Ginny's face flushed as her hand found his crotch and pressed firmly against it, manipulating his hardness mercilessly, hungrily. "Eat my tits!"

Spur switched to the other breast, taking as much as it as he could into his mouth. Tasting, then sliding back until only the hard, reddish brown nipple rested between his lips. As he ate Spur slipped down Ginny's drawers. His hand went to her fury patch and rubbed the outer lips.

Now naked, Ginny ripped at Spur's clothing, apparently unembarrassed. She unbuttoned his shirt with one hand while fumbling at his fly with the other. Spur laughed.

"Relax, Ginny. I'm not going anywhere."

"I know, but it's been so long." Then she smiled. "You are going somewhere." She took his hand, kissed it, then pressed his fingers inside her. "You're going right in there!"

Spur returned the smile and allowed the woman to remove his boots and shirt, then he unbuttoned his pants and slid them down along with his drawers. Ginny's eyes lit up as Spur's penis swung up in its full hardness.

"God, Spur, he's so big!" she said in awe. "It's the biggest one I've ever seen!" Ginny grasped it and squeezed gently.

"Come on," Spur said. "On the bed." He flipped the cards onto the floor.

"No. Not yet."

To Spur's surprise Ginny knelt before him and sucked his entire shaft into her throat.

Spur's knees nearly buckled at the incredible warmth surrounding his penis. Ginny's eyes closed as she worked on him, and Spur couldn't help but take her head in his hands and gently, slowly pump in and out of her mouth, each trust surging his passion higher.

After a few moments of this Spur pulled away from her.

"You've done this before, Ginny Burriss!" he said.

She rose and dropped back onto the bed on her back, then lifted her knees and spread them wide. Spur looked hard at her lush crotch.

"I've done a lot of things, Spur McCoy."

He moved to her then, putting a hand between her legs, parting the lips and thrusting his fingers inside her as she squirmed in delight. Spur stretched out on her body, fingering her, pressing his mouth to hers. They parted and he thrust his tongue into the woman's warm mouth, searching, probing as was his finger deep inside her. The lashing kiss ended as Ginny turned her head and Spur's tongue slipped out.

"Enough of this teasing," she said pouting. "Put it in me!"

Spur removed his finger and raised his body slightly, feeling her hands grip and guide him.

"Now, Spur; now!" She cried out in need.

Spur rammed into Ginny in one swift thrust that pushed her body higher on the bed. The woman cried out as his hugeness filled her, then gasped for breath.

"Oh Spur, yes! Yes!"

Spur pulled back, then began thrusting his entire length into her slot. His head dropped and attacked her left breast, chewing the nipple, then switched to the right one. Ginny gasped as he pumped into her, meeting his thrusts with her hips, forcing him to the fullest possible penetration.

"That's good, Ginny!" Spur cried as he rammed and bucked. The ancient bed squeaked noisily as they wrestled. Ginny threw her legs up around Spur's thighs, resting her feet in the hollow of his back. The new position seemed to transform her; a series of cries erupted from her mouth and her eyes closed in ecstasy.

"Oh, fuck me, Spur! Harder!" Ginny's breasts flushed bright pink and her body shook with an

58

internal explosion. "Oh, it's never been so good!"

Spur found it increasingly difficult to control himself as he watched the woman's pleasure continue to grow. He finally felt the old surgings in his groin.

He increased the intensity of his thrusts tenfold, his hips blurring as the sexual friction between them sent a surge of power into his loins. Spur's body jerked violently as he shot deep within her, his eyes screwed shut as she sighed and wrapped her arms around his sweaty back.

After a few shuddering seconds, locked together in an erotic embrace, Spur's body collapsed on top of her. She sighed and lay motionless under his slick, warm body, their chests fighting each other for breath.

Suddenly conscious of his weight pressing down on the tiny woman, Spur gently withdrew and lay on his side. They both rested—panting, worn out, unable to speak.

"Spur McCoy," Ginny finally said, breaking the silence of the moment. "That was worth waiting for!" Her eyes shone as she looked across the bed to him.

He planted a kiss on her bare belly and she giggled. "I have to agree, Ginny. You exhausted me."

She pouted again. "Really? I'm just getting started. Can't you go one more time?" She took his flaccid penis in her hands, rolled it, squeezed it. Slowly it awakened and grew hard and proud.

"There," she said. "I knew you could do it!"

Spur never ceased to be amazed at the sexual capacity of women. Not that he complained.

"Lie on your back," Ginny said, trying to roll him into position. As he did so she straddled his thighs with her legs, then holding his penis, slowly impaled herself on it. "Oh God! That's the heaven my fahter's always talking about—you hard and all the way up inside me!" She brought a hand down and massaged herself rapidly as she bounced up and down on him. Spur laid back, his hands behind his head, and watched the woman work herself out on him. He was tired, but not too tired to enjoy the sight of Ginny Burriss arousing herself on his body. Her full breasts bounced majestically above her, and he suddenly felt hungry.

Spur sat upright, catching Ginny around the waist to balance her, and sucked a breast into his mouth.

"Eat it, Spur! Suck on my titty!" She bounced harder on him, her buttocks slapping against his thighs with a steady rhythm—the music of sex.

Ginny's other hand dropped behind her and Spur felt her fingers on his balls—cupping, squeezing, setting his whole body on fire. Then she slid one finger up beside his penis up into herself. She sighed and arched her back twice in rapid succession, her mouth forming an *O* as she climaxed again and again, sitting down harder onto Spur's penis.

Spur cupped her buttocks in his hands, holding her a few inches off his body as she stopped bobbing, then thrust up into her until their crotch hairs intermingled. He drove it up inside her in quick, contrapuntal thrusts, his breath choking out in ragged gasps as he squeezed her soft bottom and blindly bucked upward, finally spilling his seed out in heart-stopping spurts while Ginny shivered above him.

Spur lay as if dead, his chest pounding, his penis spasming still buried to the hilt in the beautiful young woman. She slowly rose off him and dropped to the bed.

Neither spoke for several minutes while they struggled to recover from the exertion. Spur finally lifted himself up on one elbow to look at Ginny, who slept softly beside him.

Who was this woman-child? Spur wondered.

She opened her eyes then, smiled and nestled her body against his. Spur wrapped his arms around her, pressing his face down into her hair. It smelled lightly of lilac.

"I can't tell you how much this has meant to me," Ginny said. "I don't mean—well, it's not like I think we're going to get married. But these few times I can be with a man—that's what makes the rest of life worthwhile. My father—" she sighed. "He doesn't let me have any fun. If he knew I was here with you I can't imagine what he'd do." She shivered. "But let's not talk about him."

"Whatever you want."

She suddenly turned on him. "I want you to kiss me, Spur. Hard on the mouth. Please?"

She sinuously turned her body around, threw

one leg over his and moved up against him. Spur kissed her deeply and was rewarded by hearing her moans issuing from deep within her throat.

As he broke it Spur shook his head. "You're something else, Ginny Burriss."

A few moments later they dressed, then sat on the bed. Ginny bent down to retrieve her cards.

"I want to see you again, Spur. Before you leave Kearney. Okay?"

"Try to stop me," he said.

She laughed happily, her face radiant.

Then the door burst open. The wooden frame splintered and the chair bounced across the room as they stood in shock.

CHAPTER SIX

Spur and Ginny glanced up at the hotel room's door. A hefty, red-faced man squeezed into a black preacher's suit stood raging in the doorway. Wind-blown, coarse black hair, cropped close around his skull and hanging down longer against his neck, seemed to add to the man's wrathful appearance.

"Painted whore!" he spat. "Heathen slut! You'll burn in hell for this, girl!"

Spur rose. "Who the hell are you, and what are you talking about?"

"Servant of the devil!" the man hissed at Spur, then stalked across the room and grabbed Ginny's arm. When she resisted he drove his palm down hard against her cheek.

Spur's fist slammed into the man's jaw, jolting him away from Ginny.

"Are you all right?" Spur asked the woman.

"I'm fine."

"Idolatrous hussy! You'll burn in hellfire for

your lustful sins!" The man glared at them. "I didn't raise my daughter to go around—"

"Your daughter?" Spur asked. Ginny nodded meekly.

"—visiting strange men's rooms at night unescorted! It's tantamount to fornication! For the Lord saith, 'Verily, he who lies—'"

"Save the Bible quotes, Rev. Burriss. Your daughter's unharmed. Ask her." Spur cursed under his breath. He'd bedded the preacher's daughter. Great.

"You servant of Satan! Fornicator!" The big man's neck shook as he prated, the rippling flesh intensifying its reddish colors. He rubbed his chin where Spur's fist had smashed it.

Good, Spur thought. He's afraid to get hit again.

"I'll not have you polluting my daughter with your un-Christian ways!"

"Father, I—"

"Shut your mouth, whore! I'll deal with you later. Now get on out into the hall."

"But—"

"Get!" the man thundered.

"Maybe she wants to decide," Spur said. "She's not a little girl any more."

"Stay out of this, sinner! This is my daughter and she'll do what I say. Right, girl?"

Ginny nodded meekly and moved slowly from the room, frowning. She gave Spur a half-hearted smile and disappeared. She's got to break free from her father, Spur thought.

"Don't think you can come into town and bed every young unmarried woman you see. Just because you've fornicated your way across this God-fearing country doesn't mean that you'll do so with my daughter!" He stabbed the air with his finger. "Watch yourself, stranger. You're lucky I caught you before anything could happen!"

"You scare me, preacher. I'm shaking in my boots."

"Goddamn you!" Burriss roared.

"Ginny's not a helpless child. She must be eighteen, nineteen. Plenty old enough to do what she wants with or without your approval."

Fire shone in the reverend's eyes. "That kind of heathenish talk has put lots of girls into trouble, and then what became of them?"

"She's a grown woman, Burriss. You can't live her life for her. Let her do what she wants."

Burriss threw back his shoulders, closed his mouth and marched past Spur out the door.

McCoy shook his head. Ginny Burriss had one hell of a father to cope with. As much as Ginny enjoyed sex, Spur couldn't imagine why she stayed with her father. He certainly wouldn't have thought that she lived with such a man while they had been in bed together—Spur had seldom had a more enthusiastic woman.

Ginny Burriss cowered in the corner of the parlor, shielding her face from the blows the reverend rained down on her. Tears spilled freely from her eyes.

"I'll teach you to go to men's hotel rooms!" Rev. Burriss thundered. "How dare you disobey my orders! You were to stay here while I was out!" He slapped her face again. Slashes of red rose on her delicate skin, marring her beauty. "Have you been tarnished by Satan? Have you been possessed by a spirit? One that forced you against your will to do such wicked acts?"

"No!"

Burriss' face grew in hatred and blood lust. "I think so, girl. I think I know the cure. God is telling what I must do to cleanse you of your wicked nature." His powerful forearms wrapped around her waist and he easily lifted her, then lay her face down on his lap. Avoiding his daughter's blows the reverend hiked up the back of her dress, then savagely ripped the drawers from her body. "An exorcism of pain, my dear! Avaunt thee, Satan! I will drive you out by the powers of the almighty hand!"

Reverend Burriss stared down hungrily at her perfect white buttocks. He delicately caressed her bottom, then lifted his hand.

"Prince of darkness, leave this poor girl!" The hand contacted Ginny's exposed flesh with such force it squeezed out fresh tears. Ginny kicked and screamed as the second blow cracked across her cheeks, then another and another.

Burriss felt a warm glow within his broad-cloth trousers as he spanked the woman, and the tightness against his fly grew with every repetition.

"Leave this woman!"

"Father, stop!" Ginny cried helplessly, then twisted on his lap, driving her elbow into his crotch.

Blinding pain shot through the man's body;

his mouth hung open in soundless horror. Ginny broke free and scrambled across the floor, then stood.

Stunned at her luck in eluding her father, Ginny straightened her dress and faced him.

"All right, Father. You want to know about me? About the real Ginny Burriss? I'm not the woman you think I am—or the little girl. I've slept with lots of men. Dozens of them. I've seen every size, shape and color of pricks and I don't intend to stop doing so."

Burriss groaned in pain as he rubbed the damaged area. "Goddamn you! You nearly unmanned me!"

Ginny smiled. "That's not much of a job. Father, haven't you been listening to me? I'm the whore of Babylon you always warned me about. I'm one of those women who spread their legs for any man. You know why? Because it feels good—better than anything else. It tells me I'm alive, makes me feel like a woman."

Burriss face flushed. "Ginny!" He winced.

"That's right. I even made love with that man you found me with! We'd just finished." Her eyes sparkled as she relived the moments. "I tore off my clothes and then he sank it deep into me! Does it shock you, Father, your good little Christian daughter talking this way?"

"I'll have no more of that kind of talk in my house! If you've fallen from the ways of the Lord I won't keep you under my roof!"

"You should know, Father. Fallen from the ways of the Lord! You're the most hypocritical man I know." She moved her head sharply, sending lustrous black hair cascading around her shoulders. "Don't think I don't know where you go when you sneak out nearly every night!"

Burriss sputtered, then regained control. The pain had ebbed. "Where?"

Ginny was astonished, not only at the look of fear that flickered across her father's eyes, but also at her own daring. Is this really me talking, she asked herself, or was she possessed by some errant spirit? No. She was tired of her father's tyrannical ways and she wouldn't bear them any longer. Imagine the pleasure she'd been denying herself! Now that she'd made love again she knew there was nothing else in life so sweet.

"Tell me!" Burriss thundered.

Ginny paused a moment; she wasn't sure where her father went, but she had suspicions. She decided to play them out. "Peterson's. I've seen you looking at that fancy woman, Roxanna Stafford. You probably sleep with her twice a week. How much do you pay her, Father, or does she let you do it for free because you're holy?"

Burriss' face washed with relief. He halted rubbing his crotch. "Young lady, you're in a shitload of trouble now." He rose from the floor where he had sat.

"Father, swearing again!" She clucked. "Not a very Christian way to act." She frowned. "Don't you understand, Father? You don't own me anymore. I won't listen to a word you say."

"Fine. So go off and take up with strange men," Burriss said. "What happens if you get

68

knocked up? If you're been fucking so many men it's bound to happen. What then? How will you raise a baby without a husband? And what will that make you—and your baby?"

"I don't care. I don't have to, since I have this Indian herb that takes care of that." She smiled sweetly. "One day when you were gone I met an Indian woman in town, and she told me about it. She was a Christian, of course, but she remembers the old ways. I've thought of everything."

"Not quite. No man will marry you. Oh sure, they'll talk about you, probably relieve themselves at night thinking about you, but they'll never give you their name. No man will. Because you'll be a whore, anybody's woman."

Ginny burned in embarrassment for a moment, then shook her head. "I don't care. I could get a job in a saloon."

Burriss laughed heartily. "That's choice. You, a fancy lady. The preacher's daughter. It'll make me the laughing stock of the country."

"You already are."

Burriss' eyes shone with flashes of intensity. "Don't speak to me like that, hussy! You may be a loose woman, but you're still my daughter. Be out of here as quick as you can! I'm sure it won't be too hard to find a warm bed to sleep in."

"Fine with me!"

Burriss' face suddenly softened. "Ginny, I'm sorry you've fallen into these evil ways. Won't you pray with me to rid you of the wicked spirit that has set its evil grip on your very soul?" His eyes filled with paternal tenderness.

Ginny, confused, looked away from him. That was time enough for Edward Burriss to grab his daughter, shove her into her windowless bedroom, and lock the door with the skeleton key.

"Father!" Ginny screamed, pounding on the door.

Burriss pressed against it, feeling it vibrate against his body. He imagined his daughter's white buttocks streaked with pink, shaking in fright as his hand raced down toward them with ultimate authority.

McCoy woke with a grunt to greet the hot morning sun that shot directly parallel with the floor, across the bed where he lay. Spur rubbed his eyes, stretched and walked to the pitcher and basin where he splashed cold water on his face, stinging him to full consciousness, then dried with a stiff towel.

After he'd bathed and eaten three eggs, two cups of coffee and a pile of bacon in the dining room he walked to the livery stable and hired a fine looking bay horse and saddle. Just before he mounted, Spur pulled Sheriff Gardner's list from his pocket and studied it. The Circle T seemed as good a place to start as any. He pushed the paper back into his pocket, slid into the saddle and headed east out of Kearney.

Dust-laden heat suffused the bleak area. Plains stretched around him with monotonous regularity, the sky a deep blue bowl arching above. He rode easily, not tiring the horse, collecting his thoughts.

Spur finally saw the well-painted sign supported by two high posts over a gate: CIRCLE T RANCH. He went in through the gate and rode alongside pens and hay barns approaching the two story wooden structure— the largest ranch house Spur had seen. The Circle T must be doing well for the Tate family. Perhaps they'd have a lot to lose if homesteaders moved into adjacent property. Perhaps they—or Roscoe Tate, as Gardner had pointed out—were responsible for the Parker killings.

He rode past a huge corral and finally halted the bay at the hitching post outside the great house, slid to the ground and tied up his mount. Spur turned and approached the front door just as a gunshot blast rocked the house with a deafening sharpness.

CHAPTER SEVEN

SPUR RAN to the house as the sound of the shot died. He gripped a window frame and peered inside. A table, bookcase, chairs. No firearms, bodies, people. Spur bent at the waist and ran toward the window opposite the one he'd checked on the other side of the porch. Again, nothing suspicious. The Secret Service man knocked loudly on the front door.

Moments later it was opened by a plump, fifty-ish woman with blue eyes, a pinched face and a decidedly cold manner.

"Can I help you?"

"Sure hope so, ma'am. I'm Spur McCoy. I just heard a rifle blast inside the house and hoped you were safe. Has there been any trouble? Do you need any assistance?"

She shrugged, sending a few curls loose from the bun on her head. "No more trouble than usual. My sons were fighting and got too rough.

You've come at a bad time, I'm afraid. I'm Amanda Tate."

Spur tipped his hat. "Pleased to meet you, Mrs. Tate."

"So what brings you to the Circle T?" She stepped aside and motioned him into the house. "Please, come in." Amanda Tate closed the door behind him. "This way." They walked to a comfortably furnished parlor—overstuffed chairs, velvet curtains shielding out the hot sun.

"I'm here to ask about the Parker deaths last week."

The mention of the name brought color to the woman's white face. Her hands went to her throat.

"I see. Are you friends of the Parkers, perhaps family?"

"No," Spur said. "I never met Al or his family. But I've heard talk that they were killed—someone set that fire, it was no accident—and I'm trying to find out who did it. That's why I came out here to see what I could learn."

"Have you been to the sheriff? I'm sure he must have conducted an investigation." Her voice was steady, controlled, but disturbed.

Spur decided it was time to lay out his cards. "Mrs. Tate, I—"

"Amanda. Please call me Amanda."

"Amanda. I know there's been trouble between the ranching and homesteading factions of this area. I think the deaths of the Parkers have something to do with this. What do you think? After all, you live here—you might know what goes on."

She shook her head. "I'm sorry, Mr. McCoy."

"Call me Spur." He shot a smile to her.

"Fine, Spur. I don't get to town too often, and I don't follow local gossip. I'm afraid I can't be of much help to you."

"But surely you've heard something—"

"Rumors. Only rumors." She shook her head. "When I think of those poor people trapped in their house while it burned down around them . . ." She closed her eyes and shivered.

"Do you think ranchers may have been responsible for their deaths?"

Amanda Tate glanced at Spur abruptly. "You don't mince words, do you, Spur? But I hardly think you should ask me these questions; I'm just a rancher's wife."

"Then perhaps I could speak with your husband?"

"Sorry. Daddy's not feeling too well," a low voice growled behind them.

Amanda and Spur turned. "Spur McCoy, meet my son, Roscoe Tate."

The men exchanged nods.

"This your new suitor, Mother?" Roscoe asked wickedly.

"Ignore him," Amanda said. "I usually do."

"Perhaps he could tell me about the Parkers' murders?" Spur suggested.

"I'm sure he could tell you some things about homesteaders in general," Amanda clasped her hands at the waist. "Couldn't you, Roscoe?"

The man stared at McCoy. "I haven't seen you around here before."

"Just got into town yesterday."

Amanda turned to Roscoe. "Well, go on, son. Start spouting your story about the homesteaders. You know, how they're carving up the plains and ruining ranching. About how barbed wire fences cut across prime grazing land and the best drive routes. Go on, Roscoe! You've been talking about nothing else for months!"

Roscoe shrugged. "It's like she said, McCoy. I figure outside of two years they'll cut our profits way down. So much so that it's only sense to be worried about the homesteaders."

Amanda laughed. "Worried? You worry? The only think you worry about is eating and sleeping and drinking and loving! You don't care for the ranch and you know it!"

Spur shuffled his feet, feeling out of place in a domestic squabble. Amanda looked at her son for a few moments, then threw her hands up in disgust and turned to Spur.

"Trying to talk sense into this boy is like trying to convert a priest. He already shot a hole in my brand new wallpaper this morning. Roscoe, why don't you go into town and blow off some steam! You could use it, and I could use the peace and quiet!"

"I love you too, Mother," Roscoe said, then left.

Amanda sighed. "That's Roscoe."

Spur nodded. The man seemed to fit the general pattern—he definitely hated farmers. Did he hate them enough to kill them? Spur didn't know. Yet.

"Can I get you some coffee?"

"Sure. I'd love some."

Amanda sighed. "I don't know about Roscoe sometimes. It seems he's a child who hasn't grown up yet." She disappeared toward the kitchen.

Roscoe Tate walked into the bunkhouse, surprising two hands sleeping it off there. They scrambled out of their bunks, dressed only in their drawers, and faced the owner's son.

"Sir, we wasn't trying to ditch work, it—"

"Cut the shit," Roscoe said, "and put on your pants. I don't care if you work around here or not. But I've got a job for you." He took a flask out of his pocket and offered it to the men when they had finished dressing. One was Anglo, the other Mexican. The Anglo eagerly opened the flask and drank the burning whiskey as Roscoe talked.

"There's one man—at least—snooping around the ranch. His name's Spur McCoy. I don't want him or anyone else doing that. You understand me?"

The Mexican received the flask, raised it and the liquid spilled down his throat. He nodded in mid-drink.

"Why not, Mr. Tate?" the other asked.

The Mexican handed the flask to Roscoe, who wiped off the bottle and drank deeply. He then screwed the top back into place, and slipped it into his pocket.

"I don't want this ranch going up in flames! He may be a homesteader, or a gun they hired. I don't want anything harming the Circle T." He looked toward the door and saw Spur walking out of the ranch house. He motioned the two men to look at Spur.

"That's him. See him?"

"*Si.*"

"If you catch him sneaking around, checking up on things here, looking into our windows or just plain acting suspicious, let me know."

"And if we think he's dangerous, about to do something?"

Roscoe belched and ran the back of his hand over his lips and moustache, wiping them dry.

"Kill him."

Spur led his bay mare to the edge of the broad, shallow Platte River for a drink. He left the horse there, tied to a bush, then stretched out leaning against a cottonwood, thinking.

The low drone of insects permeated the afternoon stillness until he heard a splash and a feminine voice. Spur jumped to his feet and walked to the river. Five hundred feet downstream a natural depression had caused a pool of deep water to form, and in this pool Spur saw a naked woman bathing.

She lifted the crystalline water above her head to cascade down over her body, splashing off the nipples and sliding past her smooth thighs. Her body shimmered in the sunlight.

Spur wondered if she knew he was watching. If so, she didn't mind an audience. He approached the pool, hands stuck casually into his pockets, his head down low so that the Stetson's brim cut off the water's glare. She noticed him then, and smiled as she saw him drawing closer.

"Hello!" she called. "Come in. It feels wonderful."

It certainly looked wonderful, Spur thought. He debated for a moment. Not wise to turn down an invitation from a naked woman, Spur thought. As he undressed he looked at her more closely.

She was a real beauty, perfectly formed, the lines and curves of her body flowing into each other in pleasing patterns. Her skin was honey-golden in the sun, almost matching the long brown hair piled and knotted on her head. The face below it was sensuous: full, luscious lips, deep eyes, high cheekbones and just a touch of mischief.

"Get those pants off and come in here!" she said. "I usually bathe alone but I sure don't mind company."

"Do you do this often?" Spur asked as he stepped out of his pants and walked naked to the river. Despite his best intentions a partial erection swung before him. The woman's eyes widened as she watched it, mesmerized.

"God, you're packing a big piece there, stranger!"

"And you've got two fine, huge tits on you, lady!"

He entered the water and splashed ten feet to her. At this point the water level centered around their waists. Spur looked and saw her dark patch inviting him. He slipped down a hand and touched it.

"Nice! Real nice!" the woman said, and took Spur's penis into her hands, fondling it to full hardness as it floated in the water.

Spur bent at the waist and sucked in the woman's left breast, forcing as much of the warm mass into his mouth as he could, then moved back and concentrated on the nipple, sucking, licking, and biting it. The woman's hand grew more insistent at Spur's crotch and he finally had to throw it off him before he prematurely exploded.

"Watch that!" Spur said, pulling his mouth from her breast. "I almost shot my load!"

"Um. I love a man who talks dignified to a lady." She giggled and took his penis again, and pulled him toward the bank with it. "Let's go over there and do this right."

"No. I've got a better idea," Spur said. He turned the woman around, pressed her back gently so that she'd bent over, then pried her buttocks apart.

"I like the way you think," she said, shivering.

Spur guided his erection to the right spot, then bucked forward and slipped up into the woman.

"Oh yes! Ride me! Shove that thing deep in me and make me feel like a woman!"

Spur grabbed the woman's waist as he pumped into her, their bodies sending water splashing crazily in all directions. The unexpected sex, brazenly performed in the open, excited Spur more than he had expected. He looked down to watch where their bodies met and grunted.

"Oh, drive that huge thing up me!"

Spur's thighs slapped against the woman's buttocks as he pounded into her. She gave a cry and her breathing grew more erratic as he furiously thrust and withdrew. One moment her head slipped below the water but she surfaced a scant second later, coughing and pushing back to meet Spur's thrusts, forcing him deeper into her body.

Spur felt the woman tremble with orgasm and finally let go, ramming savagely into her as colors danced before his eyes, his body shaking with an internal explosion.

He thrust one last time and then pulled out from the woman. She stood and turned to look at him.

"God, that was wonderful! Just what I needed."

"We haven't been properly introduced yet," Spur said, fondling her breasts. "I'm—"

"No!" the woman said, putting her hand before his mouth. "Don't tell me your name. I never want to know that." She gripped his penis and pumped it vigorously below the water's surface. "We don't need to know each other's names, now that we've known everything else." She slipped closer to him, kissed his lips briefly, then let him go and walked toward the other side of the river.

"Hey!" Spur called, following her. "Aren't we going to see each other again?"

"No," she said. "I'm just passing through. But it was fun, and thank you for a wonderful time."

She splashed off and Spur stopped, watching her move, her buttocks gracefully swinging in the sunshine, glistening and throwing off pellets of silvery water as she ran.

Who the hell was she? Spur asked himself as he went back to the river bank and found his clothes threwn over it. He laughed and leaned back, staring straight up into the dazzling sky, at peace with the universe.

Except for those who killed the Parkers. The glow of satisfaction the exciting woman had provided to him vanished.

Who had killed the Parkers?

CHAPTER EIGHT

SPUR SWAYED gently in the saddle as he rode back to Kearny. Afternoon sun slanted across the plains before him, charging the earth with gold and orange hues. The bay whinnied a complaint and stamped a hoof into the dust-laden trail.

"Easy girl. We'll be home soon."

The horse relented and continued its pace. Spur scanned the horizon—unbroken save for a few rises or farm buildings pushed up against it. When Spur swung his gaze back to the trail directly before him, he noticed a rider approaching fast.

He didn't change his horse's gait, though all his senses were keyed to the rapidly approaching figure of a rider, horse and dust track. Someone was heading somewhere fast.

A few minutes later Spur identified the man— he was Sheriff Gardner. Where in hell was he going? Spur wondered. Soon Gardner reined in his horse five feet from Spur. The animal stamped and shook, lathered, nostrils popping with breath.

"Spur!" Gardner said. "Shit, am I glad to see you!"

"What's up, sheriff?"

"Trouble. Fred Lucas was murdered last night. Stabbed in the gut and hung until he strangled or bled to death."

Spur grimaced. "He's a farmer?"

Gardner shook his head. "A rancher." He patted his horse's neck and rubbed his shoulder. "Nope; it looks like the farmers are reacting to the Parker killing. They're returning fire with fire."

"Know of anyone who'd do such a thing?" Spur asked as the two men dismounted and stood in the center of the trail.

Gardner shrugged. "Half the farmers within twenty miles could probably be talked into killing a rancher. You know how things are."

"Yeah. Where's the Lucas ranch?"

Gardner turned and looked around him. "A half mile west of here you'll see an old burned-out farm. Turn right there and ride due north for four miles. You can't miss it."

"You've already been there?"

Gardner nodded. "I came out here looking for you, thinking you had gone to see the Tates. What'd you think of them?"

Spur frowned. "Don't know. Amanda Tate seems normal enough, but that Roscoe—"

"He's quite a character, isn't he?"

"Does he get on well with other people around Kearney?"

"No. He's pretty much a loner. Hasn't made many friends since he came back." Gardner sighed. "He's just plain ornery, if you ask me. Well, I should head back to town. You going to the Lucas place?"

"Yeah," Spur said. "You find anything there?"

Gardner shook his head. "Nope. Doubt if you'll do much better, but it's worth a try. No one saw or heard anything; a cowboy found him early in the morning, hanging from an old tree, his stomach a mass of slashed flesh and dried blood." Gardner scowled. "Who the hell would want to kill Lucas? He was one of the finest men around."

"Maybe some angry farmer who doesn't take kindly to seeing his friends get killed."

"Guess you're right; one senseless murder for three."

"See you around, Gardner. Thanks." Spur stepped into the saddle and rode toward the landmark, leaving the sheriff standing by his mount.

It wasn't a long ride but Spur had time to think before he arrived at the Lucas ranch. The next killing magnified the Kearney problem. If the farmers were indeed striking back and Lucas's murder wasn't unconnected, twice as much danger now existed for the citizens of Kearney County. He not only had to find the Parkers' murderers, he also had to discover

Fred Lucas's killer and try to halt the tensions rapidly worsening in the area.

"Great," Spur said. "My problem just got twice as complicated."

A half hour later Spur rode into the Lucas spread. It was typical of ranches in Nebraska, with several corrals, barn, bunkhouse, and a one-story ranch house, all woodframed and shiplap sided.

Seven cowboys idled the day away in the shade of a huge spreading oak that must have been transplanted from back east. One strummed a guitar, the others sat or laid back, hands clasped behind their heads, drifting on memories of earlier times, softer companions.

As Spur's approach became audible over the music the men looked up in various stages of alarm. As Spur halted his horse at the edge of the gratifying pool of shade the men relaxed. This was no farmer.

The men must be idle because their employer was dead.

"How're doing, men?" Spur asked.

"Fuckin' fine," one said.

"You work for Fred Lucas?" Spur stepped to the ground beside his mount, then tied it to a hitching post nearby.

"We used to," the same man answered. "Now we work for Mrs. Lucas, we think. What's it to you?"

A ring of nervous eyes scanned his every movement, gesture, and expression. He shrugged to ease off the tension he sensed in the men.

"I heard in town that Fred Lucas had been shot last night, and that another family—can't remember the name—got burned up in their house a few weeks ago."

"So?" a man with a thin beard shot back.

Spur shrugged again. "So I was thinking of moving into Kearney, but these killings and farms being burned up and all are making me think twice about it."

Another man—gruff, unshaven, black hair flowing onto his shoulders, moustache drooping around his mouth—stood up.

"Ain't no danger unless you're a rancher," the man said. "Shit, the farmers are behind Fred Lucas's murder. They have to be!"

"Why?" Spur asked. "Because he's a rancher?"

The area suddenly grew still. The long-haired cowpoke faced him squarely, his left eyelid twitching.

"What's wrong with that, stranger? You wouldn't be one of those homesteaders, would you?"

Four more men stood, hands placed jug-handle style on waists or tensely held into fists.

"No. I'm no farmer, but I'm not a rancher either. Fact is, I'm a lawyer. That's why I'm interested in Fred Lucas's death—the legal aspects of it."

"You don't look like no laywer to me," said a Spanish-accented voice with a high, nervous sound.

"Why the hell don't you go back where you came from?" said a white-haired, grizzled old hand who'd probably worked twenty spring drives.

Spur felt the tension increase. The men were outraged, scared. If he said the wrong thing he could set them off like firecrackers.

"Yeah! Get the hell off this ranch!"

"Enough!" a high voice said behind Spur. "I've had all I'm going to take of this!"

Spur turned and saw a stunning woman approaching, her head held high, half-shrouded by a length of black lace that hung down from a simple hat. Her firm, enticing body was tightly wrapped in a black dress accented with black lace and jet buttons which travelled its entire length.

Her clear, calm face with prominent cheekbones, languorous blue eyes and fine, full lips peered out from behind the veil that partially obscured it.

"That'll be the last outburst of poor hospitality I'll ever hear on the Lucas ranch. Do I make myself clear?"

The men grunted their assent.

"Mrs. Lucas?" Spur said.

"Yes. I'm Lorna Lucas." She extended a hand.

Spur grasped it for a few seconds. "Spur McCoy."

"You're here to inquire about my husband's death?" she asked with a steady voice. Her eyes betrayed no emotion.

"That's right, ma'am. If it wouldn't be too much trouble."

"Not at all." She turned and dismissed the men with a flip of her chin, then held out her arm for Spur to hold as they walked to the simple frame house.

Lorna Lucas couldn't be much past thirty, Spur thought. Her fine bearing and features betrayed a heritage of careful breeding and vast quantities of old money. Her skin was so fair. Scandinavian? Spur wondered.

"I don't know how much I can tell you," Lorna said, as they strolled. "My husband was asleep—at least, I guess he was." She smiled briefly. "I hope you won't take offense at this, but I didn't sleep with my husband. We had separate bedrooms. So, I'm assuming he was attacked in his sleep, dragged out there, and then killed."

"Did you hear anything unusual last night or early this morning?"

"No. I slept right through to five-thirty, my usual rising time. So you see there isn't much to tell."

"I'm sorry to put you through this again, Mrs. Lucas."

"It's nothing. I'm used to blood and pain and death. I'm just not used to it happening to my husband. It was so—" She paused a moment. "Unexpected? Death always is, I suppose."

"And you saw no one or nothing around his body to betray the murderers?"

"Absolutely nothing. They'd ridden off long before his body was found—hours earlier. I'm sorry if you've wasted your time coming out here," she said. "But let's have a glass of sherry and talk." She suddenly clasped his hand. "I need to talk to someone now."

Spur nodded, meeting her earnest gaze with calm, self-possessed eyes. Delighted, she led him into the house and to a glass of dry sherry. The wine wasn't the best quality, but he didn't turn down offers from beautiful woman. Ingratitude had never been Spur's style.

They talked for a half hour, general chatter, Spur thought, then he politely excused himself and left. After poking around the farm for a few minutes, and investigating the place where they'd found the body, Spur rode back to town.

He tied up the bay before Peterson's and walked in. His throat was dry from the ride. He also knew from Gardner's list that this was a good place to catch Jack Parsons.

Parsons was a rancher who'd been vocal in his opinions concerning homesteaders and their use of barbed wire, Gardner's list had told him. Parson's ranch lay three miles east of Kearney, but he might as well talk to the man while he was in town, at least get a chance to sum up the man. Parsons usually hit Peterson's around noon when he came to visit friends in Kearney, and apparently did so nearly every day.

Walking into the saloon Spur knew he could pick out the face if he wanted to waste an hour or so, but when he saw Roxanne decided to save time. He walked over to her and she smiled up at him from the table over which she was slumped.

"Hello, Spur. Nice to see you again. Are you ready?"

He smiled. "Maybe later. Do you think you could tell me something first?"

Roxanna pursed her lips, then spread them expansively. "Anything you want."

Spur turned around one of the straight-backed chairs, straddled it, and moved closer to the table opposite Roxanna. "Tell me if Jack Parsons is in this room. Don't make it obvious, but if you'd point him out I'd appreciate it. Could you, Roxanna?"

"Sure. But what do I get out of it?" She pouted gorgeously. "I mean, when I do a man a favor I expect him to do me one back." She batted her incredibly long lashes a few times, then straightened her back and thrust out her huge breasts. "See anything you'd care to do a favor with?"

Spur laughed. "Lots, Roxanna, but I don't have the time right now. I'll owe you one. How's that?"

She sighed. "What are you, a preacher? One of those Bible thumpers like old man Burriss? Let me tell you, Spur; that's not the only thing he thumps!"

"Roxanna, please," Spur said, touching her wrists acorss the tabletop. "I need your help."

"Okay. Now, where is he?" She raised a painted fingernail to her lips as she searched the room. Moments later she turned back to Spur. "I've found him. He's at the first table, the one closest to the door, wearing a brown hat and beige shirt. A tall man with a moustache."

Spur spotted him. Parsons didn't seem to notice the attention he was receiving. The man drank and smoked continuously, pouring shots from a whiskey bottle and pulling cigarettes from a pile of the neatly rolled sticks.

Spur turned back to Roxanna. "Thanks. I owe you one."

"Hey! That's two you owe me!"

"Fine. I appreciate your help." Spur pushed off the chair and walked in Parsons's general direction. He'd decided not to talk to the man at that time—he was too drunk to be of much good. But he could test the man nonetheless.

Beside Parsons's table Spur feigned tripping and landed directly on Parsons.

"What the hell?" Parsons yelled, then shoved Spur off him as he stood and glowered.

"Excuse me," Spur said in a slightly intoxicated voice. "I tripped."

"I guess you did! Why don't you watch your feet, clodhopper!"

Parsons's somewhat handsome face was streaked with sweat that burned down his flushed cheeks. Brown hair and browner, red-veined eyes; a tall, lanky build just under six feet; hairy arms and chest where it showed through the beige shirt and black vest, made up the file on Jack Parsons.

"Sorry," Spur said, brushing off his shoulder.

"Keep your goddamned paws off me!" the man bellowed. "You'd best get the hell out of here, stranger! I'm in no mood for clumsy fools!"

"I apologized. You'd better be happy with that, 'cause that's all you're going to get from me."

"Then leave me alone!" Parsons stuffed the

cigarettes into his vest pocket and grabbed the bottle. He moved to another table and sat, his back toward Spur.

McCoy grunted and exited the bar before anything more could occur. One thing was clear —Parsons was hostile. If Parsons was one of those guilty of the Parkers murders he may by now know Spur was poking around town checking up on things—others must know by now.

That could make things tougher.

CHAPTER NINE

THAT NIGHT, bats flapped across the inky sky, their bodies and furry wings silvered by the moon. Owls spoke from tangled bushes and rose in a flurry of activity, while below a snake slithered across the cold sand.

One hundred feet from the snake a circle of twenty masked men rose suddenly, their already hushed conversation cut short by the unexpected sound. Two scouts broke from the group and wandered slowly into the surrounding terrain.

"Nothing," one of the two said as they returned.

The men settled before the fire again. Around them cottonwoods stretched their branches sixty feet up. The natural copse marked an underground water source—probably a runoff from the Platte River. It also formed an ideal setting for clandestine meetings. Lovers had coupled there, rustling the leaves with their passionate gyrations. Tonight the men who gathered there showed desperation on their faces. In dim flicker of firelight—screened by the trees, the men themselves and the undergrowth—they talked.

One of those who sat back, thinking, not participating in the talk was Thomas Standler. He didn't belong here. He didn't want any part of this meeting, or the men running it.

He looked at the leader. He thinks he's so tough, does he? Thinks he can clear all the homesteaders out of the Platte River Valley. He'd do that even if it meant killing every one who wouldn't move.

Standler himself had been suffering because of the fencing and the formerly free-to-use grazing land. Some of his best had been taken from him less than a month ago. Still, he'd seen bad times before and had weathered them. Standler figured he'd do so again.

"We've got to wipe them clean off the plains!" the leader said, a big man with a gruff voice, his face hidden with a kerchief as were the other men's. The man's eyes reflected the fire's meager light as he continued to talk. His guttural voice was forceful, but quiet. This gathering didn't want uninvited guests stopping by. "They're going to kill the cattle business if we don't do something about them! We'll all be on our butts, broke, if we don't get rid of them now!"

Standler sighed. This guy's tune never changed. He'd been droning on and on like this for at least an hour. He didn't recognize the man. He almost had the voice pegged but not quite. Standler was there because he had to be, not from worry about the homesteaders.

A friend of his had stopped by his ranch that afternoon, telling him to be *in the copse* one hour after dark. Thomas tried to put off the invitation, but he man seemed angry about his hesitance. The meeting was for the protection of the ranchers, the man had explained. Didn't Standler care about his ranch? Gary had the distinct impression that if he didn't attend the meeting he'd be sorry later.

Now he didn't know where all this would lead.

"Fred Lucas was deliberately killed in cold blood last night, by some damned asshole farmer tryin' to break our spirit. Well, we won't stop bothering them until they're gone from our land!" The man's voice grew in volume. "They won't scare us off!"

"I thought Lucas got killed in retaliation for the Parkers," someone in the gathering said.

The leader's head turned toward the speaker, his eyebrows low. "Who said that?"

No information was volunteered.

"Goddamn you!" he said. "Forget the fucking Parkers! They're dead and gone. Let's concentrate on getting the rest of the homesteaders out before they destroy our ranches. Hell, any of you who're soft on the farmers should get the hell out of here. Right now. We don't need your kind, and I'll deal with you later."

A few grumbles and grunts ran through the assembled men but they soon died. Thomas

Standler knew he should speak out, make a stand or leave. But here among his fellow ranchers he sensed the safety of a common cause. However he felt about the homesteaders, he couldn't disagree with the leader that ridding themselves of the sodbusters would work to all their benefit. He was afraid if he stood and walked away he'd be shot as a traitor to the cause. So he sat, lost in the circle of the men, and thought.

"What's the next move?" one rancher asked.

The leader jumped on the question. "Another burning. This time we'll be sure no one gets hurt. We'll hit a farm—one I'll choose at that time. I wouldn't want the farmers forewarned. We'll herd them outside, burn down their house and maybe a few other buildings, then tell them to move or we'll kill them. Simple as that. That should be enough to send them scurrying back east as soon as they can find transport." He laughed, a low, dirty laugh. "And good riddance to them."

"What if they don't leave?"

"Then we hit another farm."

"Do we kill the farmers of the other place, like you said we would?"

The leader shrugged and grasped one hand in the other before him. "That depends. Leave it to me."

"Who killed the Parkers? Was it an accident? I'm still not clear on it." The question was anonymous.

"Shut your goddamned mouth!" the leader spat. "Don't ask stupid questions! I'll need

98

three good men to do the job. It'll be tomorrow morning. Any volunteers?"

"Why the hell ain't you going?" one man asked.

"Come on, men. I need three volunteers to ride out tomorrow morning, put a scare into a family, and torch their place. Sounds like a lot of fun, right? Who wants to do it?"

No hands raised. After a few seconds, he nodded. "Then I'll have to find some men. As for you men—act normally. We won't have another meeting unless tomorrow's strike goes bad. Everybody understand?"

The men nodded assent.

Thomas Standler, though, did not. A doubt throbbed in his mind, one that chilled him. He didn't think the Parkers had accidentally been killed, and the leader had done nothing to quench his fears. Thomas thought they'd been killed, and that that had been the plan all along. Why the smokescreen, though? The leader was obviously the type who enjoyed killing—at least as far as homesteaders went.

"When the farmers move we'll make them pack up that barbed wire and take it with them. We don't want it here! And we'll stamp their crops into the dust and everything will be back to normal. I can feel it, men; I can feel the day when the ranchers once again rule the valley, and the tall grass stretches out unbroken on all sides."

Thomas smirked. Not likely, he thought. Not if the homesteaders were bold enough to kill Fred Lucas. At this rate, they'll kill each other off and no one would be left in Kearney County but the merchants and the sheriff.

Will the next homesteading family be killed? And if so, who will be the next ranchers to follow him into hell?

Thomas shivered. He didn't like this business at all.

Carl Lanford dropped his pants and drawers, then climbed onto Roxanna and thrust into her.

"Hey, watch it, big boy!" Roxanna said, wincing in pain. "You've got a thing bigger than most of the men in this town put together!"

"Shut up, Roxanna. I'm thinking." Lanford's mind was preoccupied while he enjoyed the woman's warmth and moist tightness. Though his hips moved mechanically his mind raced in other directions.

It was their move now, he thought. Now that Fred Lucas was dead the ranchers and farmers were even. He was certain no farmer would raise a hand against a rancher until it was clear the ranchers weren't going to leave them in peace.

The thought of the Parkers brought renewed vigor to his strokes. Roxanna groaned as he filled her to capacity, then nearly slipped out on the backstroke. His sharp, bony knees pressed against her soft skin, raising bruises where they continually banged against her. Lanford's sweat mingled with hers as he strained to work out his problems.

Lanford suddenly lowered his gaze to Roxanna's face, now transfixed with pain and ecstasy. Furious at the interruption, he pulled out and slapped her thigh.

"Turn over," he growled.

Roxanna moaned and lifted herself heavily up, then over. Lanford took her waist in his hands and pulled her into a kneeling position, then rammed into her from behind. Roxanna sighed as he sank in.

Now less distracted, Lanford was barely conscious of his intimate connection with the woman. Nothing like sex to clear your head, he always said.

Lanford banged into Roxanna and mulled over his problem. Being a farmer, the ranchers threatened his existence. If he was faced with death at the hands of the ranchers, he'd welcome the opportunity to take down as many of the bastards as he could before he dropped to the ground.

Not that all ranchers were bad, Lanford thought. Sure, some were the meanest sons of bitches you'd ever care to meet, but others were downright friendly. A few were worse than others, he thought grimly. At least his troubles in that area were now over.

Lanford had done his part in harassing the ranchers—all the farmers had been talked into it at one time or another. He had to admire people who could stand up to the treatment they'd received.

He remembered the men who'd shot him dirty looks in the street, or the time he'd found a threatening note tied to the carcass of his favorite dog, or the morning he'd found his chicken coop blazing away—chickens prematurely roasting loudly within it.

He could kill them. Easily, one by one. Lanford's attention switched to the present, to the woman he thrust into. She squirmed beneath him as their bodies slapped together.

Lanford finally groaned and slammed into Roxanna with such force she fell to the bed. The man's buttocks thrust crazily as pleasure spread through every nerve in his body, his mind's eye filled with images of his enemies' bloodied corpses.

CHAPTER TEN

SPUR ATE in the Calico Hotel's dining room, then walked outside into the cool evening air. The street was quiet—Kearney wasn't a thriving city—so he climbed the outside hotel stairs and sat at its top, leaning back against the railing, letting his thoughts drift as he digested his meal.

McCoy found a cheroot in one pocket and stuck it between his teeth, then lit a stinker match and soon had its tip glowing in the darkness. He inhaled and slowly blew the biting blue smoke into the air.

"Spur!"

The voice cut through the night. He jumped to his feet and searched the area. No one was visible.

"Spur McCoy!"

The voice was high—a woman, or a young boy.

"Who wants to know?" he boomed into the

darkness. Still no signs of life. If the voice wasn't echoing and bouncing off several buildings, it could be originating from his right.

"I have a message for you," the voice continued, now directly behind him. Spur sprung around, only to realize the voice had echoed off the hotel's wall.

"Show yourself!" he called.

"No."

The word was followed moments later with a small heavy object dropping to the dirt before the stairs. He raced down them and crouched over it. A piece of paper had been tied around the rock.

Crude, Spur thought, but effective. He picked up the rock and strained to hear the sound of departing feet, but detected only silence. A search would be fruitless.

He returned to his position at the top of the stairs and broke the twine, then unrolled the paper. Spur had to move over two feet to use light from a nearby hotel room's window to read. The lettering was in an unschooled hand:

Meet me in back of Petersons in one hour.

No name or indication of its sender. Spur frowned, crushed the paper, threw it and rose, then stood looking at the door. Roscoe? Spur thought. Or Jack Parsons? What about some other rancher who didn't like Spur nosing around the place? It could also be a farmer with news, or perhaps someone totally unrelated to the murders.

Spur drew heavily on the cheroot and finally turned and walked down the stairs and into

Peterson's. If he had to meet the unknown party behind the saloon, he might as well slip in a little early and check local sentiments concerning Fred Lucas's untimely death.

Peterson's was noisy and dusty, stank of tobacco and stale whiskey and sweat. McCoy got a drink and stood at the bar, listening as conversations drifted past him.

Most of the men discussed matters of daily living; Spur head the words *horse*, and *herd* frequently. The fifteen men situated around the saloon drank, smoked and talked, but Spur heard no mention of Fred Lucas's death.

McCoy casually ambled around the saloon, as if he couldn't find a comfortable place to sit or stand. Once he'd heard the subject of the conversations around him he moved on.

After the fifth or sixth such move the name Lucas stood out above all the rest of the words.

" . . . got shot last night."

"You're joking," another voice said.

"No. You didn't hear? Lord sakes, it was all over town."

"Tough. Lucas didn't deserve it."

"Hell no!" the first man said. "I think it was some damned homesteaders, if you ask me!"

Spur moved to look at the men. One, lean, tall, smooth-shaven over a hard jaw, had a gun tied to his leg. He spoke again.

"Maybe. We'll never know for sure."

"Sheriff Gardner just didn't try hard enough!" a bright-eyed younger man said. "I'll bet ya we could find out who killed Lucas better'n any lawman."

The older shook his head. "How you gonna do that? You don't have the time or the brains."

"I got everything I need. It was a farmer, right?"

"Could be." The man swallowed the last of the whiskey in his glass. "I don't know."

"And you don't care, right?" The younger man gripped the other's vest at his midsection. "Look. Lucas died at the end of a rope. You wanna be next?"

"Get your hands off me," the older man said sharply. The other complied. "Of course I care, Kenyon! I'm no fool. But I don't see what getting upset about it's going to do. Now leave me alone; I've got some thinking to do." He turned way from the other man.

"Wise up, Waters!"

Spur idly turned from the men as Kenyon walked away. Kenyon and Waters—the two names were on Gardner's list, possibly trouble-makers. Could be something. At least he'd have to keep the men in mind when he had more evidence or information regarding the death of Fred Lucas.

Spur estimated a half hour had elapsed since he was summoned. He put his drink down and wandered out the back door and into the night air. An alley stretched behind the saloon, with a row of mostly one-story buildings abutting it on both sides. The alley was dark save where moonlight slanted in between shadows. A perfect place for a meeting.

He quickly chose the best spot to wait; one with his back to a solid wall where his vision was unblocked by buildings. Spur moved up against the brick wall that must've been the rear of a store or office building and settled against it, preparing for the wait.

Fifteen minutes later he heard a scuffling in the dirt down the alley ten or twenty yards to his right. Someone walking—clumsily. He waited.

Moment later the scuffler came into view—a woman. In a flash of moonlight Spur recognized her—Roxanna Stafford, the saloon fancy lady.

He relaxed then—she couldn't be the contact. Roxanna stepped into the middle of the alley and looked around her. Spur froze. Was she the one who'd summoned him there?

"Roxanna?" Spur said from his hiding place.

"Yes?" She clutched her bosom, looking around her. "Who's there? Is that you, Spur?"

"Yes." He stepped from the shadows into the light.

"Good. Got my note, I take it?"

"Yes."

"I wondered if I'd paid that boy a nickel for nothing, but I guess he was honest."

"Roxanna, what's this all about? Why the note and all this secrecy?"

"Because it excites me," she said. "I like to be in dangerous situations with handsome men."

"I see. What did you want to talk to me about?"

"Not here. Let's sneak up the back stairs and go into my room. No one will see us, so no one will suspect us."

"Of what?"

Roxanna shook her head. "Never mind. Come on, lover boy!" She held out her hand. Spur took it and they walked to the stairs, climbed them side by side, and went into Roxanna's room.

"Whew!" Roxanna said, laying a hand on her ample bosom. "That just makes me tingle!" She shivered and moved her body back and forth, gently falling into a swaying motion while her gaze locked onto Spur's eyes.

"Fine. Let's talk. That is why you wanted to see me, isn't it?"

She halted and frowned. "All right, Spur McCoy. I can see I'll never get you in my bed. And it's not just the money I'm thinking about, Spur. Honestly. You're—you're kind of nice."

Spur smiled. The woman seemed sincere. At least she loved her work.

"Okay. I asked you here because I heard you were looking for information."

Spur feigned innocence. "Information? About what? What gave you that idea?"

"You know what I'm talking about," Roxanna said. "Information regarding the deaths of the Parkers."

Spur shrugged. "Maybe."

"Don't worry," she said, flapping her hands before her. "I won't give away your secret. I don't know why you want to know about the Parkers, but you do, don't you?"

Spur nodded. "How'd you know?"

"I hear a lot in my line of work," she said, then smiled. "Men like to talk after doing it, you know? Anyway, this afternoon a customer mentioned that you were snooping around, trying to find out as much about the Parker killings as you could."

"So?"

"So, a week ago another of my customers was a cowboy. He'd been out riding range and saw three men riding toward the Parker ranch. It was early—just before dawn—on the day the Parkers were killed."

"Three riders?" Spur asked.

She nodded. "He was too far away to see faces. I asked him if he did, because he seemed interested in it. He was convinced that they'd been the men who'd killed the Parkers."

"What about the men's clothing, hat types, perhaps their horses?"

She shook her head. "I asked him that too, just out of conversation-making, but he didn't see anything more than three riders heading toward the Parker ranch."

"Did he see them come back by there later that day?"

"No."

"When did he tell you this?"

"Wednesday, last week. One week after the Parkers were killed."

"What was this cowboy's name?"

"I don't know." Roxanna blushed and turned away from Spur. "I don't remember their names too often, unless they're regulars—you know. But I'd remember that guy if I ever saw him naked again—he had the biggest one I'd ever seen."

Spur walked to the woman. "Do you know

which ranch he worked for?"

Roxanna thought for a moment, then turned back to Spur and shook her head. "I'm sorry. He was just one of the many, not too special except below the waist. He wasn't staying in town, anyway; said he was going back east on the train." She shook her head. "I think he said that." Then her eyes lit up as she looked at him. "Does that help you out?" she asked eagerly.

Spur didn't disappoint her. "Some. At least I know that three men hit the Parkers—as long as this guy was reliable, not just lying or deliberately spreading false information."

"Why would he lie? No. Men don't usually lie right after—unless it's to tell you they love you. They spill their guts on everything. Hell, they tell me things they wouldn't tell their wives or closest friends."

"I see. Thank you for the information, Roxanna. It might help out."

"With what you're doing? What are you doing here, Spur? Why are you in Kearney?"

He shrugged. "Just passing through."

Roxanna crossed her arms on her chest. "If we'd just done it, you'd tell me everything."

Spur laughed. "If we'd just done it you wouldn't be able to talk for five minutes at least."

"I'd sure like to find out," Roxanna said, laughing.

Spur smiled and turned to look out the window. The alley was quiet. A second later he felt a hand on each side of his waist, then they travelled down to his crotch and pressed against his penis.

"I'll promise you anything," she said. "If you'll just get that damned thing out!"

Spur firmly but politely removed the woman's hands as he turned. "Not now, Roxanna."

"Okay, Spur. I give up. You've got to be the stubbornest man around. I know you're no priest—seems like you and Ginny Burriss had a fine time together—but I guess you just don't go for me."

"Where'd you hear that?"

"About you and Ginny? I hear everything." She looked at him pointedly. "And if I hear more about the Parker killings and I think you'd like to hear it, I'll let you know."

"Good." Spur bent and kissed Roxanna's cheek. "Thanks, Roxanna. You're quite a lady."

She smiled and caught her breath. "Sure, Spur. Goodnight, and thanks for coming."

Spur moved out of the room, down the stairs and back into the alley.

Three riders. If the source was reliable—and Roxanna may have a point about men opening up right after sex—that meant he had to find three men. Of course, if he found one, the other two would be easy to uncover.

As he walked down the alley to his hotel, moving through alternating areas of shadow and moonlight, Spur heard a faint sound behind him.

Three steps later, he heard another.

A kicked stone. Leather scraping dirt. The presence of another human being behind him. Someone was following him.

CHAPTER ELEVEN

JULIUS CRAIG coughed twice to quiet the room, then stood. Twelve men eyed him from various positions in the cramped Craig parlor, and the man sweated. He loathed public speaking, feared and hated it.

"Gentlemen, let us begin."

Craig was a homesteader who had brought his wife and daughter to farm in Kearney County over a year ago. His twelve months of hard farm work had done little to diminish his round face and somewhat rounder body. Thick brown hair sprouted from the man's tanned head and lower face, which had been tamed into muttonchop sideburns and a full moustache which hid his upper lip. His conservative dress —denims, white shirt, string tie—belied the informality of the occasion. His friends had wanted to gather, and Julius Craig happened to have the largest house.

Craig tapped his right hand against his leg as he continued.

"Someone killed Fred Lucas. Someone else killed Al and Gilly Parker and their child. Obviously, we have a real problem here." Craig's fear pulsated in his stomach. He tried to push it away but it lingered.

"Now, I don't know who killed Lucas—I certainly didn't do it—and I don't much care either. I'm sorry to see any man killed, of course, but sometimes . . . ah, things become necessary." Craig's face flushed and blood rushed through his veins and arteries at an accelerated pace. "So tonight I thought we could talk about this and—perhaps, ah, come up with some ideas."

The farmers stared at him, waiting. He had to get the meeting going.

"Ah—ah—"

"Ah hell!" Carl Lanford sprang to his feet. "Craig, I'll take charge here, if you don't mind."

"No. Not at all." Craig gratefully sank back into his chair, his face crimson.

"Good. Now, we all know how bad a year we've had—the locusts coming in and nearly wiping out some crops, the drought, the storm that destroyed the wheat—it's just been one thing after another for farmers in Kearney County."

"Damn straight," an older man said.

"Now we've got another problem; not another drought, or swarm of gasshoppers. No. It's the ranchers. They could be worse than anything else we've had thrown in our faces.

114

"Fred Lucas is dead. Who killed him isn't important at this time. What is important is that this'll probably stir up more trouble with the ranchers. As sure as hell one of us—or one of our neighbors or friends—is going to get hit by the ranchers. As you well know, they're far past stampeding through crops and tearing down fences. New they're burning down homes and killing women and children." His face was grim as he paused. "It's up to us to stop them before all this gets out of control."

"How in hell you going to do that?" a young man of twenty-two asked.

"I don't know!" Lanford boomed. "That's why we're calling this meeting, so we can come up with some ideas. You have thought about this, haven't you?" Lanford caught each man's gaze singly. "What else has there been to think about?"

"My daughter's getting married next month and I—" one middle-aged man began.

"I don't care about your daughter's wedding!" Lanford screamed. "Not when our lives are at stake! If you get burned down some cold morning you won't have to worry about paying the preacher! Now, any ideas?" Lanford planted his hands on his hips.

Murmurs rippled through the assembled men, but no one voice stood above the others.

"Nothing?" Lanford asked, then shook his head. "Then I guess this doesn't mean anything to you. Great. It's me against them, right?"

"Of course not, Carl," Craig said, rising. "We're all worried—otherwise we wouldn't be here. But worry doesn't always bring solutions. We don't know what to do. Frankly, Carl," he said while biting his lower lip, "we thought you had some plan in mind."

Lanford gazed silently at Craig for a moment, then smiled and cocked his head. "All I can think is to keep watch every night. Hire someone, if you can afford it, or use your young, but have someone alert at all times to stop trouble before it starts."

"What about me?" An older man with a bad eye asked. "I'm all alone. How am I supposed to keep watch?"

"They probably wouldn't touch you, since your farm is so small, Pete."

"We can't afford to hire an extra hand just for that, or let our hands have any less sleep," another man grumbled.

"Goddamn it, men!" Lanford said. "That was only a suggestion."

"What about Sheriff Gardner? Can't he do something about this?"

"Look what he did for the Parkers," someone said.

"There is an alternative." Lanford's voice rose above the others. "We could use their methods."

Craig looked sharply at Lanford. "What in hell are you talking about?"

"Shut up, Craig." He turned back to the men. "It's the only real solution; why didn't I think of it before? We do the same things they're doing to us—to scare them away."

"It won't work," one man said.

"Why not?" Lanford shot back. "What makes you an authority on this? Anything can work if we try hard enough. If we don't do something they'll force us out of the valley. They're scaring you, aren't they?"

"Someone wasn't scared," Pete said. "Someone killed Fred Lucas to avenge the Parkers."

"That's right," Julius Craig said. "Lanford, I don't like what you're saying. Oh, I'm no man of peace but I do know when something's wrong. I'll have no part of your *ideas*, and I won't allow you to spread them in my house!"

"Watch yourself, Craig," Lanford said. "Some day you'll wish you were my friend."

A general ruckus had broken out during the verbal confrontation. Men talked in groups of two or three.

"We'll burn down all the ranches in one week," said one.

"Stampede their cattle so far they'll never find them," another called out. "That way they'll have to leave."

"After that I don't see them giving us more trouble," a gray-haired man said to himself. "Nope, I just don't see it."

Lanford broke from the argument with Craig and stomped his foot four times to silence the men.

"So it's agreed. We'll strike back! We'll show them who rules Kearney County!"

"No!" Julius Craig said. He laid a hand on Lanford's shoulder and shook it. "That's not the way! We've got every right to be here—as much as they do, by God. They simply have to learn

117

that the old ways are gone forever—they've got to stick to their own property, or pay us for passage over ours. This has to be the only solution, the only sensible one. Lanford, you're just asking for trouble."

Lanford brushed the man's hand off his shoulder. "You know we can't teach those ranchers anything. They won't listen to us. Why can't you see that? Stop being so stubborn."

"They're reasonable men. Surely they can see the truth. They have to give in. Let's call a town meeting and get the ranchers and the homesteaders together and work out our problems! We have to stand together, man to man."

Lanford laughed. "Listen to him! Are the ranchers going to listen to us? Hell no. We'll be talking our hearts out while they set our families and farms on fire!" He stared at Craig, then spat in disgust.

Julius watched as the mucus splattered onto his best rug, then looked at Lanford, raging.

"Get the hell out of my house, Lanford! Get off my property! Now!"

Lanford had already turned to leave and didn't acknowledge the man's command. Instead, he clapped another man's shoulder as he walked out.

Julius Craig stood at the end of the room, watching as one man after another rose and walked out with Lanford. Soon only Pete remained in his chair. He rose and moved across the room to sit beside Craig.

"We'll convince them, Julius," Pete said softly.

Craig sighed. "I hope so, Pete. I hope so. Lanford's not really a bad man—just temperamental. I thought—never mind. Let's pray that these men come to their senses."

Spur ducked into a foot-wide alley between two buildings, blending with the shadows as he waited for his pursuer to make the next move.

Spur calmed his breath as he felt for his Colt. Yes, it was still there, ready when necessary.

No noise from the alley. From his position he could see three feet to either side of the alley's walls, and no shadows moved there. The scuffling noise had halted.

Spur tensed, wanting to spring out into the alley, to show himself so that this follower would have to do so as well. But he waited, straining to hear the slightest sound.

Footsteps lightly peppered the ground, moving toward the side alley's mouth. Seconds later a figure moved directly before the opening and passed on, apparently oblivious to Spur's presence. Though it was dark, Spur didn't have to guess that the figure was a man, and that he wasn't the one following him.

McCoy waited five more minutes—nothing. He edged toward the intersection of the two alleys and, after unholstering his Colt, poked his head out from the passageway and waved its barrel back and forth.

No answer.

He moved closer and looked out into the alley.

Nobody in sight.

Spur shrugged and, cautiously, walked into the alley, then turned to his right and moved briskly down it toward the hotel. The man following him must have slipped away.

A second later a large figure burst out from a shadow and blasted lead at Spur. The man's aim was off; the rounds slammed into a brick building, chipping it into dust and ricocheting off crazily.

Spur returned fire, but his rounds did no more than force the man back into the shadows. McCoy ducked behind a water barrel and waited. He detected a flicker of movement and aimed but realized the shadow led into a passageway between two buildings. The man was gone.

He jumped up and ran back a few feet until he found the next passage to the other side of the buildings. Pounding the dirt with his heels Spur made it to the street just in time to see the man rush out across Main Street's eighteen-foot breadth and duck into yet another lane. Spur followed and just as he ran into the blackness he froze—the man was on the ground, face down.

Spur approached him cautiously and kicked the man's legs. Had he tripped and hit his head on a rock, or was he faking?

McCoy turned the man over with his boot toe while aiming two-handed at the downed man's heart. The corpse suddenly leapt into life, raising the pistol he'd hidden with his body.

McCoy's booted foot smashed into the man's hand, sending the gun skidding twenty feet along the dirt. Spur crashed his foot against the man's chest, knocking him flat onto the dirt, then stared down at him.

"Who the hell are you?" Spur asked.

The man shook his head. Spur smelled his boozy breath and felt him shivering beneath his foot. Drunk and scared. Maybe he'd get information from him after all.

"Why are you following me? Who hired you?"

Again the shake of the head. Spur stared down at the man, his face barely visible in the dim light. He was young, Mexican, no more than nineteen.

Spur cocked the Colt and pointed it at the young man's face. Instinctively, he moved back. The man's head hit a wall and he slowly pushed himself up into a sitting position, leaning against the brick wall. Spur's eyes never left him.

"I'll ask this once more, *señor*," he said calmly. "If you don't answer this will be the last thing you'll ever hear." He nudged the Colt's muzzle against the man's ear.

"He'll kill me," he said. The voice was tight and lightly accented.

"I'll kill you right now if you don't tell me what the hell I want to know! At least I'll let you go after you tell me, and you'll be able to make a run for it, maybe escape. Who hired you?" Spur moved the gun from the Mexican's ear and pressed it against the soft skin in the man's neck.

He seemed almost ready to talk, then fear gripped him. The Mexican shook his head.

Spur savagely dug his boot heel into the man's groin. He groaned and bent double as Spur retracted his foot.

"Talk!" he thundered.

"Okay. Okay!" He moaned once more and rubbed between his legs. "It was Tate," he said, his voice clear and strong.

As Spur's mind raced a gunshot rocked the alley and light flashed a split second before the Mexican's upper body slumped forward, his head bouncing on the dirt between his legs.

CHAPTER TWELVE

SECONDS AFTER pounding two bullets into the
end of the alley, Spur heard feet moving rapidly
away. He bolted forward, unwilling to let his in-
formant's murderer escape.

He ran out of the side alley into a larger one
at the rear of Main. As he moved his mind
worked. Tate had someone following him.
Which Tate? Surely not Amanda. That left
Roscoe.

Hell, Spur thought. Maybe the man was angry
at him for poking around the ranch. Perhaps he
even thought Spur was sent there as a spy by
the homesteaders.

Then again, Roscoe Tate—or one of the Tates
—may be responsible for the Parker murders,
and didn't want Spur uncovering anything. It
was a possibility.

Spur waited for signs that he had been
followed. When none came, he was confident it

wasn't a trick this time—the man who'd killed his pursuer wasn't coming back.

The agent moved slowly down the alley, then switched to Main Street. He didn't want any more alleyway confrontations that night. Moments later he walked into his hotel room at the Calico, locked the door, tipped his hat to the floor and slept fitfully. He didn't even bother pulling off his boots.

"What the hell are you talking about?" Roscoe Tate thundered. He stood on the front porch of the Tate ranch, barefoot, wearing his underdrawers. It was nearly midnight. "Who told you to follow him in town?"

"No one," the hand answered sheepishly. He was twenty, with a full moustache and beard, close-cropped black hair, lazy eyes and a stupid grin spread over his face that screwed up his eyes. "But we was there, drinking and talking about fucking Roxanna, if we had the money. Well, we needed to piss so we went out in the alley. Who should we see but Spur McCoy? We hid out until Spur had passed us, then Lopez started following the man. I told old Lopez I was tired and was going on back inside, which I did. Then I heard a couple gunshots and so I ran back outside—when I got there Spur had Lopez on the ground in an alley, gun to his head, asking him who'd hired him to follow him. Before I could do anything Lopez said, 'Tate.' I didn't know what to do, so I shot him."

"Who?" Roscoe asked, glancing sharply at the man.

"Who?" the man repeated.

Roscoe punched him in the stomach. "Who'd you shoot?"

"Lopez," he said between coughs and groans.

Roscoe reflected on this news for a moment, ignoring the man's pain. "Is he dead?"

"Yes.'" A cough. "I'm sure of it. After I shot him I didn't have much time to check; I just ran. Hid out in Peterson's until closing time, then rode out here."

Tate nodded. "You always were a good shot. That damned Lopez was a fool. No great loss, him. Thanks for your help, Young. Expect a bonus real soon."

The man's face glowed in spite of the throbbing in his gut. "Really? Thanks, Mr. Tate. I figured I had to kill him, even though he only said *Tate* and didn't say which one."

"Nothing else you could have done," Roscoe said. "Besides, Spur McCoy might have thought Lopez was lying to save his ass. If McCoy gives me any trouble I'll be sure to return it doubled. You have any other news to report?"

"No."

"Good. Then let me get back to sleep! I've got to be up early in the morning."

"Fine. Thank you, sir."

The man slipped off the porch and Roscoe closed and locked the door behind him. He walked barefoot back to his room on the second floor, glad that the hand had had the sense to throw a pebble against his window, rather than waking the whole household. He didn't relish the thought of his family knowing his actions—yet.

Tate closed his bedroom door and got back into bed. He stared at the ceiling, wondering what the coming day would bring.

Spur jolted upright in bed, awake instantly as the doorknob's jiggling broke the stillness of his night-drenched room. He fell to his back, motionless, on top of the blankets. Every nerve in his body was alert, ready. He maintained a low, regular breath pattern to disguise his wakefulness.

He waited for two minutes. Spur saw darkness cross his curtained window, then watched as the shadow of the window's center frame slowly crawled upward, rippling against the curtains where they hung in regular folds.

Spur moved his right hand a fraction of an inch closer toward the Colt .45 strapped to his right thigh. The bed creaked.

The shadow halted in perfect synchronization, then continued on to the top. The curtains bent inward for a split second, then fell back to reveal a man climbing through Spur's window.

He half-closed his eyes and continued to watch the proceedings, wondering who it was this time—and if he was from Tate, too.

With his back to the window, the intruder was nothing but a black outline against a lighter background. He was big, though—Spur could see that, well over six feet. Curly hair stuck out around the brim of his Stetson, and McCoy heard the click of spurs as he crossed the floor to the bed.

At the right moment Spur's fist smashed into the man's face, breaking skin and fracturing some thin cheek bones.

The man fell backward as Spur jumped to his feet and drew the invader's six-gun from his holster. Spur came up with both pistols trained on the man's chest.

"Wait!" the man said, whispering. "Don't shoot me, for chrissakes!"

"Why not?" Spur asked. "You were going to shoot me."

"Did I have my pistol out?" the man asked shakily, still in a soft voice.

"No," Spur said. Something was strange here. "What are you doing, then, sneaking into my room in the middle of the night? That's a great way to get yourself killed." Spur hadn't lowered the weapons.

"I was delivering a message," he said. "I wasn't supposed to kill you, just scare you into leaving Kearney County. Honest, that's all."

"Why?"

"So you wouldn't set up law practice here," the man said, with a deadly serious expression.

"What?" Spur asked, then remembered the story he'd told the cowboys at the Lucas ranch. Word sure got around quick. Or was this a bluff? "Who told you to scare me off?"

"I don't know. I really don't!" His eyes were glassy with fear; his voice still quiet. "I just got slipped an envelope by someone in a crowd at the train station this afternoon. I couldn't figure out who'd given it to me. Inside it was a note and a twenty dollar bill." The man swallowed. "Hell, I'd do nearly anything for twenty dollars."

"Why didn't you just take the money and run?"

"The note said they'd kill me if I didn't do what I was told to. They said they'd be watching."

"That's why you're whispering?" Spur asked.

He nodded. "I don't know where they are."

Spur frowned. "Do you still have the note?"

"I brung it with me so I wouldn't forget what to do." He felt in his pockets.

"You can read?" Spur asked.

The man shook his head. "I had a friend of mine read it for me, but I can make out some of the words. And I sure as hell didn't have no trouble finding someone to read it—as long as I was willing to split the money." He continued to dig into his pockets.

"I see. Tell your boss—if he ever contacts you again—that you did just what you were supposed to do."

He smiled and produced a much-folded piece of thick paper. Spur read by moonlight streaming in through the window.

"Evans, here's $20. If you want it, go to room 201 at the Calico Hotel and rough up the man there. Don't kill him, just scare him off. We'll be watching. If you run, you're dead."

The note was unsigned.

McCoy handed it back to Evans. "Now get out of here. If I ever see your ugly face again I'll blast you into so many pieces it'll take a week to get you back together again!"

"Yes sir!" Evans said, then walked to the window.

"Forgetting something?" Spur asked.

"Huh?" The man turned around just in time to catch the pistol Spur had thrown to him. He slid it back home. "Thanks."

He was gone.

Spur closed the window, then lay back down in bed, slipping his hands under his head. Things were getting stranger and stranger in Kearney, Nebraska.

An hour before dawn Spur was up. He stripped off his shirt and undershirt, splashed cold water on his face and chest from the basin, then dried and redressed. Fully awake now, Spur tugged on his coat, clammed the hat into position, slung the Spencer repeater over his arm, and left the hotel. He retrieved his horse from Peterson's and mounted. Spur turned east and soon was beyond the last buildings of Kearney. Even the train tracks veered away from the east trail and so he was soon completely isolated as he rode toward Julius Craig's homestead.

Since he had come up with so little on the Parker killings so far, Spur decided to check on the homesteaders nearby to see if one of them had killed Fred Lucas. Spur also needed to know what kind of man Lucas was—perhaps he'd had many enemies and his death wasn't linked to that of the Parkers.

As Spur rode, his horse's nostrils shot out trails of steam into the morning air. He didn't know what to make of last night's skirmish. If Roscoe Tate was guilty of the murders he might have put a man on Spur to follow him around, to make sure he didn't get too close. But then again, Tate might have done it simply because he didn't like Spur, or because he was threatened by all the farmers in the valley.

And the man may have lied, thinking Spur'd let him go if he said any name. But the Mexican in the alley had been afraid, and Spur knew that fear nearly always ensured truthfulness, unless an even greater one awaited.

Evans was another matter. The man's story, plus the corroboration provided by the written note, seemed to indicate that the man wasn't lying. But Spur knew he could have been faking —the note could have been written and the explanation worked out before, in case he was caught.

Then Spur wanted to kick himself for not thinking of something earlier. When he'd asked Evans why he'd been hired to scare him, Evans had replied that it was to keep Spur from setting up law practice.

The note hadn't mentioned that little fact.

Spur hunched over his horse in an effort to warm himself and puzzled it out, trying to get his bearings by the landmarks that the sheriff had given him. There's the red barn. That should be the place. He turned down a lane between fields of new wheat greening the rich earth. As he approached the house he heard a distant shot — apparently coming from Craig's place. Spur pushed the horse to its limit, flying past the fields toward the house. Three men rode before it, firing into the air, then aiming their weapons toward the house itself.

Another attack by the ranchers? Spur grimaced as he raced toward the house, digging his heels deeply into the horse's flanks.

CHAPTER THIRTEEN

SPUR SPED toward the Craig farmhouse, hoping the attackers were too busy to spot him. A quarter mile from the house he leapt from the bay, ground-tied her to a rock, then ran toward the house, his Spencer firmly gripped before his body with both hands.

The men apparently hadn't noticed his approach. He moved in to within two hundred feet of the house, then knelt and aimed at the closest rider. Just as the man lifted his rifle Spur fired, slamming a round into the man's chest. His body jolted backwards off the horse and bounced on the hard-packed earth. The horse galloped away from the house.

Spur ducked behind a pile of straw and waited a second, then darted forward fifty more feet. One of the attackers rounded the house and reared his horse back as he saw his downed companion. He glanced wildly around, pausing long enough for Spur to pound two rounds into the man's chest. Blood spilled out and the attacker's face was awash with confusion as he slumped forward, the rifle falling from his lifeless hands.

Two down, Spur thought, as he ran closer to the house, using a wagon as cover. He moved laterally, settling in behind the well. The third rider stormed up, apparently aware of the situation. He fired wildly, aimlessly in all directions, completely mystified at the source of his companion's executions, then turned and blasted four rounds into a window. Spur heard a scream inside as the glass's shattering subsided. Spur fired once—the shot went wide.

The gunman turned toward Spur and peeled off one round as he rode behind the barn for cover. Spur reloaded the seven shot Spencer and watched from his position behind the well bricks. A minute later he lifted his head above the well to watch the barn. A round hit the water bucket rope, sending the wooden pail crashing down into liquid blackness. Spur fired twice at the barn but had no target. A moment after his fire was returned, he bolted from the well to the other side of the house. No rounds answered his action. Spur walked quietly, avoiding leaves and branches around the house, stopping when he could see behind the barn.

The man hunched there spotted Spur at the same time. The agent bent slightly at the knees as he fired the Spencer, spitting two rounds toward the gunman. The unaimed shot went wide, but Spur's next round ripped through the man's skull, smashing his brain into jelly. With a wailing scream the figure crumpled to the ground and lay still.

Silence returned as the last detonation echoed in the stillness of the morning.

"Hello?" a male voice called from the house.

"Yeah!" Spur yelled. "You all right?"

"We're fine, thanks to you."

Spur made it to the front porch and found a middle-aged man and a young woman of perhaps eighteen standing arm-in-arm, half afraid to step outside the door.

"Julius Craig?" Spur asked.

The man nodded. "I'm afraid you have the advantage."

"Spur McCoy."

"Pleased to meet you, Mr. McCoy," Craig said, and pumped his hand. "Lordy, I don't know what we'd have done if you hadn't showed when you did."

"Do you know why anybody'd want to do something like this to you?" As he asked the question, Spur's eyes darted toward the younger Craig. She gazed at him then, for a moment, her face a mask of passion. Her eyes held his with a hypnotic power that Spur found difficult to resist. With great control Spur forced his eyes and attention back to Craig's words.

" . . . probably ranchers, I'd say. We've been having a lot of trouble last few days." Craig smiled broadly then. "You haven't been introduced to my daughter, have you? Spur McCoy, this is Leah Craig, my pride and joy."

Leah curtsied slightly and smiled. "Pleased to

meet you, Mr. McCoy." Ringlets of rich black hair cascaded down her back, swaying gently as she moved. Her face was tanned, eyes large and clear, her nose strong but not too prominent. Incredibly long lashes dusted her cheeks as she blinked at Spur, then dropped her gaze to his crotch.

What astonished Spur most was her clothing. She was dressed plainly for farm work—denim pants, a man's work shirt, boots. But the way the cloth molded to her body told Spur much of the real woman lurking beneath the masculine exterior.

"Nice to meet you, Miss Craig."

Craig coughed, regaining Spur's attention once again. "This sure is a coincidence," he said. "I was just talking about this kind of thing last night."

"Really?"

"Yeah. Had a big meeting here at the farm, all the homesteaders who cared to come, talking about the ranchers and the threats they've been making against us."

"Sounds like those threats have become realities," Spur said. "What was the meeting's outcome?"

Craig shrugged. "Nothing. It broke up when old Carl Lanford got up and started yelling all kinds of ridiculous things. Everyone left and that was the end of the meeting." Craig led Spur to the parlor.

"Would you like some coffee, Mr. McCoy?" Leah asked, poised to move to the kitchen.

"That'd be fine, Miss Craig."

She smiled briefly and moved away with a fluid grace despite her trousers.

Craig and Spur sat in rail-backed chairs in the parlor.

"Lord, Mr. McCoy, I don't know that I'd still be breathing if you hadn't come by and saved our skins," he said, shaking his head as if he didn't believe it had happened. "They took us completely by surprise. We'd been up for over an hour, of course, but we were both inside and the hands were out mending fences over on the south side all morning. We were all alone and they could've killed us."

"Glad I could be of help," Spur said. "Now I'd like you to help me, if you can."

"Gladly!" Craig said, a gleam sparking his eyes. "Name it. I owe you my life—so does my daughter," he said as she entered the room with two cups of steaming coffee. She handed one to Spur and the other to her father.

"Tell me about the situation here in the valley. What's going on? Why were you attacked this morning?"

Craig shook his head. "I wish I knew. I guess it's just greedy ranchers."

Spur set his coffee down on a table. "Speaking of ranchers, maybe you wouldn't mind looking at the bodies outside to see if there's anyone you recognize?"

"Not at all," Craig said, rising. He also set his coffee down and then turned to his daughter. "Stay here, Leah. I don't want you seeing those men."

"Aw, daddy, I'm a big girl now. I—"

"Stay here!" he said warningly, and she nodded and sat beside a portrait of her grandfather and sighed, folding her hands in her lap.

Craig and Spur went outside. They approached the first body and Spur tore off the kerchief from the man's lower face.

"No. Never seen him before," Craig said, bending to look closer at the face.

"You sure?" Spur asked, surprised. If the man wasn't a rancher, who was he?

"Positive. Let's check the others."

Moments later, Craig had studied the other two and saw no one he knew or recognized from town. "I don't understand it," he said, puzzled. "Why would anyone but ranchers want to attack me?"

"Does this mean the men who killed the Parkers might not have been ranchers?" Spur asked.

Craig shot him a glance. "Say, you seem to know local history pretty well." He thought a moment. "I don't know. Maybe."

"Unless they hired some guns to do their dirty work for them," Spur suggested.

"Could be. Well, nothing more to be done about it now. I'll just ride into town and tell Sheriff Gardner what happened here this morning."

"Don't trouble yourself," Spur said. "I'll be heading back there soon enough."

"Would you take some late breakfast with us? Leah should be just about ready to put it out."

Spur recalled that he had smelled food in the house. "Sure. I'm grateful for it."

"We can't do too much for you; not after saving us today. You didn't have to risk yourself for us."

Spur shrugged and they walked back to the house.

The meal was fine, and Spur dug into a thick steak, buttered early potatoes, and eggs fresh from the henhouse. Halfway during the meal Spur felt something warm and wiggling press against his crotch. Leah Craig, seated across the table from Spur, watched her father intently as he told his story, and laughed at its conclusion on cue. Spur fidgeted in his chair as the foot continued to caress him, soon producing an erection.

Spur reached down and pushed the foot away, alarmed that the girl's father might notice. Leah gave him a hint of a pout as she retracted her foot, but nothing more.

After the meal, while Leah washed up the dishes with water heated on the wood-burning stove, the two men talked. When Spur decided to leave Leah was nowhere to be found, so Spur shook hands with Craig and went out the door.

As he walked the two hundred feet to where he'd ground-tied his horse he heard a *pssst* to his right. Spur looked and saw Leah Craig standing in a shed, waving to him. Spur started moving directly toward her but she waved him away, then sketched a circle in the air with her hand. She wanted him to circle around and come to the shed from where he couldn't be seen from the house.

Spur nodded and walked on toward his horse,

mounted up and pretended to ride off. It didn't take more than a few minutes to find a field near the shed full of five-foot-high sunflowers. He ground-tied the horse there and made his way to the shed. Not seeing Leah in the doorway, he moved inside and shut the door.

"Hello." Leah lay naked on a homespun blanket spread out on some hay. Sunlight splashed onto her exciting body where it seeped in through warped wallboards. Spur's eyes riveted on the lustrous black patch of hair between her legs. She parted them then and arched her back, thrusting out large nippled breasts.

"Hi," Spur said. He knew what Leah wanted. He hurriedly undressed and then flung himself onto the woman, their naked bodies slapping together. Spur ground his penis against her groin as she gripped his thighs with her legs, lifting her feet to wrap them around his legs.

"Oh Spur, I knew you'd help out a poor farmer's daughter," she said rapturously as he kissed her neck.

His hands sought out her breasts beneath his chest and squeezed them, then his fingernails flickered over her nipples, causing them to harden. He lowered his mouth and sucked one.

"Ah!" Leah said. "Suck it, Spur!"

Spur savored the breast, filled his mouth with it.

"My father always told me this was the best way to spend time, or rather that it would be when I was old enough. And he was right! Every time a man lays on top of me I realize just how right he was!"

Spur lifted his head. "You've done this before?"

"Of course." She smiled, sunlight catching her face, making it glow. "I used to watch the animals around the farm while they were mating, and asked my father. He always told me anything that I wanted to know. I sure am glad."

"So am I," Spur said, then thrust his tongue into her mouth and sought out hers.

She returned the thrashing kiss, gripping his neck with one hand to pull his mouth down harder on hers, and pressed the other between their bodies where she grasped his hardness.

The kiss ended as Spur nibbled her ear.

"Put it in me! Please, Spur, put it in!" She frantically rubbed him as he continued to push it against her belly.

He rose slightly and she removed her hand as he gripped the base of his penis, then pointed it at the perfect angle for entry. Spur watched her eyes as he pressed just the head into her.

"Oh, God, Spur! More!" she cried, as her lashes fluttered and her face broke out in a sheen.

Spur inched into her slowly, then hit home. Leah sighed, and Spur realized she'd been holding her breath. He felt good, strong, horny.

"You like that?" he asked, moving his body slightly to both sides while still fully penetrating the woman's body. "You like me inside you?"

"Yes. Oh, yes!"

Spur withdrew quickly, then rammed his entire length back inside. Leah moaned and her body jerked in response.

"What about that?" Spur asked.

"Yes. Yes!"

Spur knew the woman was enjoying it. He decided a little sexy talk might increase her pleasure. He certainly couldn't complain so far about his own enjoyment.

"What do you want me to do?" he asked, staring into her fathomless eyes as they pressed together at the crotch, motionless.

She returned his gaze, then looked away, turning her head. "I want you to fuck me," she said in a low voice.

"What's that?" Spur asked, holding back from thrusting crazily into her. Each passing second increased his lust.

"I want you to fuck me." The voice was louder, but not by much. Leah wouldn't look into Spur's eyes.

"Look at me, Leah. Tell me what you want me to do."

Unbridled lust flashed over his face then, and snapped her head back to meet Spur's gaze unflinchingly.

"I want you to fuck me. Fuck me like an animal. Please, Spur; you're driving me crazy!" She reached out and pressed down on his buttocks, trying to force a deeper penetration.

"That's what I wanted to hear," Spur said. He

142

reared back and thrust for all he was worth. Leah sighed and moaned, her breath coming in ragged gasps, their bodies bouncing together and briefly parting, their connection never quite breaking.

"Oh, Spur, fuck me! Like the animals . . ." Leah said in rapture. She groaned and shook as orgasm after orgasm rocked through her body.

Spur pounded on, raising himself on hands planted on both sides of his head. He kissed her passionately as he thrust into her yielding flesh, his tongue mimicking the movement in Leah's warm mouth.

Moments later Spur's control broke and he jetted his load into her in heart-stopping spurts while his body trembled and shook, his hips jerking wildly forward, forcing himself to the maximum depth as the orgasm washed over him.

Spur lifted his sweat-drenched body from hers, shivering in the coolness of the shaded shed. Leah looked up at him dreamily as he stood naked before her, stretching and reaching for his clothing.

"Not yet," she said. "Do you have to go so soon?" She rose to her knees and pouted.

"I have to. I've got to report the killings to Sheriff Gardner. He won't like it if I don't get back there soon."

"Couldn't it wait just a bit longer?" Leah moved toward him on her knees, then bent her head toward his crotch and took his penis in her mouth. She sucked luxuriously.

Spur felt the pleasure spread throughout his

body like electric shocks. "Well, maybe it can wait a few minutes," he said as she cupped his testicles with one warm hand, squeezing them gently as she sucked.

Leah's lips slid along his shaft, coaxing it back to full hardness.

She worked with eyes closed dreamily, occasionally looked up at him.

Spur glanced down, watching himself disappearing into her mouth and felt his knees going weak.

"Leah, Christ, that feels good! Don't stop! Whatever you do, don't stop!"

She pulled her mouth from him. "I won't. And don't you stop. Just go ahead and shoot it off. I don't mind."

Spur took her beautiful head in his hands. As she opened her mouth he guided his erect penis in between her lips, then gently pumped in and out of the velvet-soft, warm and liquidy mouth.

Leah took Spur's thrusts, one hand clamping down on his buttocks to control the depth of his strokes. As Spur began groaning she redoubled her efforts, really working away at him, letting his erection slide down her throat as far as Spur could ram it. She was amazing, Spur thought.

Her hand at his balls squeezed harder, her fingernails gently scraping the sensitive skin. Spur could feel his control break; the woman's mouth was too inviting, hot, needing.

As the Secret Service man banged into her mouth he pulled her head toward him, ramming down it. Leah took it like a pro. Finally Spur let out a yell as his hips became pistons powering back and forth, spitting out his seed into her throat, again and again, finally subsiding, pulling out. He slipped from her mouth and leaned back against the wall, panting. When he opened his eyes he saw Leah Craig still kneeling before him. She licked her lips, stared at his red swollen organ as her hand moved rapidly between her legs.

CHAPTER FOURTEEN

Spur McCoy made the trip back to Kearney in little over a half hour. He rode directly to Sheriff Gardner's office, tied up the horse before it, and stormed in.

He surprised a young man leaning a chair back on two legs, feet crossed and heels placed in the center of Gardner's desk. At Spur's entrance the boy jolted forward, quickly slipping his feet to the floor. A deputy, Spur thought as he looked at the untried, wrinkle-free face.

"Sheriff Gardner in?" he asked.

"No. He's out somewhere."

"When'll he be back?"

"Don't know." The boy's wan face, accompanied by a rich head of blond hair, gave him an insipid appearance. "He said he'd be back when he was back." The boy smiled briefly, showing a broken front tooth.

"Thanks." Spur turned on his heel and strode

out, then moved left and walked along the slightly warped boardwalk, hunting in stores and on the street for the sheriff. He had to report the incident at the Craig farm.

Spur swung his gaze down an alley and saw Gardner standing above a sitting figure who clutched a whiskey bottle in his hand. Gardner was obviously preaching to a town drunk.

Spur paused a moment, planting his hands on his hips, just as Gardner looked up and waved. McCoy motioned back and within seconds the sheriff approached him.

"Ned's not all bad, but he's a slave to the bottle."

"Gardner, there's been trouble at the Craig farm."

He shot up his eyebrows. "Trouble? What kind?"

"Three masked riders attacked the place just as I happened to be riding up there this morning. The men shot in windows, yelled and raced their horses around. I picked them off one by one and neither Mr. Craig nor his daughter were hurt."

The older man blew out the breath he'd been unconsciously retaining. "When you said—I feared that Julius and Leah had been killed like the Parkers."

"No. Though they might have been if I hadn't been there. Craig didn't recognize any of the men; they certainly weren't ranchers from the area, he said."

"Strange. I wouldn't expect that. Who else would be bothering the Craigs?"

Spur shrugged. "Someone could have hired outside guns to do the job."

"Possibly. Looks like I'd better ride out there," he said wearily. "My horse threw a shoe last night. I hope she's put back together by now." He turned to Spur. "Could I ask you to do a favor?"

"Name it," Spur said instantly.

"Stop by my office and tell my son where I'm going?"

"That's your son?" Spur thought of the blank-faced young man.

"Yes. The yellow hair comes from his mother's side—all of it." He clapped Spur's shoulder. "I'd appreciate it."

"No charge."

Gardner smiled broadly and turned toward the livery stable. Spur walked back to the sheriff's office.

Roscoe Tate gripped his whiskey-filled glass shakily, his cheeks burning with rage, as he stared into the square framed mirror in his bedroom at the Circle T.

"Incompetent fools!" he muttered, then downed half the amber contents of the glass.

"It was your idea," Jack Parsons pointed out from the door.

"Goddamn you! You know we couldn't take the risk again. The first time, fine. We caught them by surprise. But this time the farmers have been warned." He lifted the glass again and watched as the last droplets flowed into his mouth.

Parsons closed the door and sat at the desk in the sumptuously appointed bedroom. "Keep your voice down," he warned. "You don't want your family hearing this kind of talk."

The man swung around. "I don't give a goddamn what they think!" he blurted out, but his voice was quieter. "Jesus H. Christ, I can't believe I was so stupid!"

"No," Parsons said in a low voice as he crossed his legs. "We just hired bad men."

"What happened?"

Parsons sighed. "I don't know for sure. Apparently they made it there—but they didn't come back. About an hour ago word got back to me that they'd all been killed."

Roscoe snorted. "Not by that damned peace-loving Craig, certainly. Did he hire any protection?"

"I don't know. But it's not too likely. He doesn't have much extra money now."

"Then how the hell do you explain the way he killed all my men?"

"I don't."

"Goddamn that fuckin' Craig! Why's he making it so hard for me to get him out of my way?"

"I doubt if the attack'll scare him off," Parsons observed.

"Of course not!" Roscoe paced for a few seconds while Parsons sat quietly. He knew how the man worked; after six months' association he'd had time to discover how Roscoe's brain worked. In a few minutes, he was sure,

Roscoe would have another perfect plan. And he wouldn't interrupt the man's thinking if he could possibly avoid it.

In a moment, Roscoe turned and moved toward Parsons, stopping a few feet from the chair.

"There's only one thing we can do to show those damned farmers that we mean what we say, and to get rid of Craig."

"And that is?"

"Hit the Craig farm again."

"What? After what happened this morning?" Parsons asked in surprise. "Where'll you find men stupid enough to do a job like that?"

Roscoe grinned as he looked into Parsons's eyes. "We'll do it. The three of us. Like last time. And we won't just scare them off."

Parsons uncrossed his legs and stood. "What are you saying?" he asked. "That we kill Julius and Leah Craig?"

Tate didn't flinch at the incredulous tone of Parsons's voice. "Of course. What else can we do? If we kill them—and destroy their farm— it'll be the last thing we'll ever have to do here. Hell, I know about your past, Parsons. Don't be so surprised at this. You haven't kept your nose clean, and you certainly don't mind sending men to their maker."

"But women?"

"There's that bank in Cheyenne, wasn't it?" he said, slowly approaching the man. "The banker and that woman, the mayor's wife, who died that afternoon. You killed them."

Their gazes locked then, Roscoe's eyes piercing points of light projecting out with palpable force, Parsons's glazed with fear.

"You're already a woman killer."

Sweat squeezed out along Parsons's forehead and flowed from his armpits. "That was years ago. I was twenty-one. I didn't kill the woman on purpose." He wiped his forehead shakily. "And besides, no one ever proved I did it."

"Yeah?" Roscoe's face turned grimmer. "How about the little rustling business you had?"

Parsons stepped back a few feet. "What the hell are you talking about?"

"Don't play stupid with me, Parsons. I'm not even sure you've quit that. How come you add two thousand head a year?"

"I've accounted for that," he said.

"Not to my satisfaction! Just think what the other ranchers would do if they thought you were the one rustling around here. They'd chop off your balls and feed them to you, then stake you out to dry in the sun, food for the foxes and scorpions."

"No! You wouldn't think of doing a thing like that to me!" he demanded. "I'm your goddamned partner!"

Roscoe smiled. "Of course I won't." He spread his hands out as if in surprise.

"Not if you help me out tomorrow morning," Roscoe said icily. "What the hell's wrong with you, Parsons? We already killed the Parkers."

"That was accidental," Parsons said,

trembling. "We went out there to scare them off—"

Roscoe's laugh halted his words. "You fuckin' idiot! I had no intention of leaving the Parkers alive. Didn't you know that?"

"You never said—"

"Some things are taken for granted." Roscoe paused and paced again. "We'll do it tomorrow morning—the way it should have been done *this* morning! We'll have to go into town, of course —to let our partner know."

"What time?" Parsons had resigned himself to participating. It wasn't that he disliked killing, he told himself. It's just that he knew the Craigs—not well, but he'd talked to them in town. He remembered Leah Craig then—the curve of her hips beneath the work pants she wore, the heavy breasts hanging in her blouse.

"Parsons, you with me?" Roscoe asked. He snapped his fingers before Parsons's enraptured face.

"Huh? Oh, right, Tate." He laughed. "I was thinking about Leah Craig."

Roscoe smiled evilly. "She's a looker, ain't she? It's a shame—shit, we've got to do it."

Parsons laid his hand on Roscoe's shoulder. "Maybe we could kill old man Craig but take her and keep her somewhere, for our own use."

"I knew you wanted to bed her, Parsons. I saw you hungering for her one day in town."

"Why not?" he asked defiantly. "I'll bet she's downright pretty in women's clothes."

"Or out of them."

"Come on, Roscoe! Why not put her up in a sod house or a shack somewhere?"

"It'd be a shame to kill her," Roscoe said in agreement. Then he shook his head. "Too dangerous. She might escape and turn us in."

"We'll see," Parsons said.

Roscoe shot him an angry look. "I'm in charge here. Got that? I make the decisions, the rules."

Parsons blinked in surprise, then nodded. He removed his hand.

"I'll decide about the girl later. We'd better ride into town. We'll show those fuckin' farmers what they get when they kill my men!" He scratched his crotch. "And maybe I'll get Roxanna for a half hour or so."

Roscoe's bedroom door flew open and David Tate walked into the center of the room.

"What the hell are you doing here, little brother? Need help wiping your butt?"

"I'll say this once, and only once. Leave the Circle T within twenty-four hours. You are no longer welcome here."

Roscoe couldn't believe it. Parsons stood in shock looking at Roscoe's younger brother.

"I've decided you're a threat to Father's health and a nuisance to the smooth operation of this ranch. Therefore, you've got twenty-four hours to move out."

"You son of a bitch!" Roscoe threw a fist toward David's stomach, but the man blocked the punch and powered one against Roscoe's jaw. The older brother stepped back, dazed, as Parsons went for David.

"No!" Roscoe yelled, coming back to his senses. "I don't need your help!"

David stood his ground, tensed, waiting for the next blow.

"You have no right!" Roscoe said. "Who's idea was this, anyway? The old man's?" He threw two punches toward David, who easily deflected them.

"I've warned you," David said. "Get off the ranch. By tonight, if you know what's good for you. There's no place for you here." He turned and swiftly left the room, his boots clicking on the hardwood floor.

Roscoe raged and rubbed his chin.

"So, I guess tomorrow morning's off?" Parsons asked.

"Bullshit it is! If I can't stay here I'll go somewhere else." He stepped closer to Parsons. "Could I spend a few days at your place?"

"I don't know," Parsons said.

"Only for a few nights. Christ, we're partners. Maybe you could talk me into snatching Leah like you planned, and I could take her with me when I leave."

"Where are you going?" Parsons had long secretly wondered exactly what the man's plans were. "And what would that have to do with Leah?"

Roscoe shook his head. "Don't change the subject. Will you or won't you?"

Parsons sighed. "Okay. For a few nights. And tomorrow morning's still on?"

"Yes, you goddamn fool! Of course it's still on!"

Parsons paused a moment, his voice lowered. "And we still kill Julius Craig?"

"Of course." Roscoe took a carpetbag from a corner and threw in essentials, all the money he had in the room, and then closed the bag.

"Let's go," he said. "I've seen enough of this place to last me a lifetime."

Parsons followed Tate out of the room, down the hall, and then the stairs. They walked directly past Amanda Tate, who stood near the kitchen entrance.

"Roscoe!" she asked, rubbing pie crust from her hands on the apron tightly wrapped around her waist.

He walked on out the front door.

"Roscoe Tate, come back here!" she said sternly.

As they moved to their horses, Roscoe scowled. "I should kill my brother!"

"If you did, who'd inherit the ranch?"

A gleam slipped into Roscoe's eyes. He stood before his mare and looked at Parsons, then laughed shortly. "I was just thinking about that myself."

"And?" Parsons asked.

"Me."

CHAPTER FIFTEEN

SPUR McCOY noticed two men riding into Kearney—Roscoe Tate and Jack Parsons, he soon realized. Spur ducked into the general store as the men passed by, then followed them, turning his head if either man looked back in his direction.

The men rode out of the business district of Kearney into the broadly spaced streets with clapboard houses standing in neat rows. Two or three of the homes were built of bright red brick that glowed in the hot afternoon sun.

As Spur walked lazily behind them, they stopped before an impressive home, one that Spur quickly recognized as belonging to Rev. Edward Burriss—someone had pointed it out to him. Spur frowned, leaned against a wall, and pulled a cheroot and a stinker match from his shirt pocket. He lit the thin, fragrant stick and inhaled as the men disappeared into the structure. What would Roscoe Tate and Jack Parsons want with Rev. Burriss?

The preacher ushered Tate and Parsons into his home quickly, almost frantically. Fortunately, Ginny was locked in her room. She wouldn't be able to hear them, he thought.

"Christ almighty!" he said after the two men were safely inside, the door shut against prying eyes. Dark drapes hung before the windows, making the interior of the Burriss home dark and cheerless. "What'd I tell you about coming here in the daytime? Anybody could have seen you!"

"Cut the crap, Burriss," Tate said as he walked into the man's parlor and sat. "What if someone saw us? What the hell's wrong with that?"

"I guess it's just that I'm nervous." Burriss's face was pinched with strain.

"Got a drink, Burriss?" Parsons asked.

"Of course," he said absentmindedly, then walked to the cupboard, took down a hidden bottle and poured three whiskeys.

"We've got some more work for you to do," Roscoe said as he accepted the drink.

Burriss looked down at Tate nervously, then sank into a velour backed chair. He shook his head.

"No. Not again. I won't do it, Roscoe. It's too dangerous."

Tate smiled. "Shit, that's just what Parsons said. You're not turning yellow on me, are you, Burriss? You haven't fallen back into the faith, have you, Burriss? That would make things difficult. For all of us."

"No. Of course not." As he spoke panic crossed his face. "What—what kind of work?"

"I wouldn't want you to have to forfeit your share in all this," Roscoe said.

"Speaking of that," Parsons said. "Just how much money do you think you'll finally collect from this scheme of yours?"

Tate shrugged. "I don't know yet. That's my problem, not yours."

"What do you want me to do?" Burriss asked, nervous at Roscoe's lack of response.

"And how do we know you won't run out on us?" Parsons asked. "It'd be easy for you to take the money and leave us here without giving us one thin dime."

"Relax, Parsons." Roscoe smiled and wiped his mouth. "You know you can trust me. Before I head out of town you'll get your fair share for helping."

"Roscoe, I demand—" Burriss began.

"How will David's announcement change your plans?" Parsons asked.

Roscoe shot him a look. "You ask too many fucking questions, Parsons."

Burriss looked from one man to the other, and decided to try a new approach. "What's this? What annoucement?"

"David's thrown Roscoe off the ranch," Parsons said, grinning. Roscoe took a quick swing at Parsons and missed.

"Watch your fat mouth, Parsons!"

"He threw you off the ranch?" Burriss said.

"Won't that make it harder for you to—"

"No. Not at all. Hell, if I have to kill my brother to get it, I will."

"I thought you'd already taken your *inheritance*," Burriss said.

"I did. But as it stands now, if my brother and father die, even if my mother is alive, the ranch legally comes into my hands."

"What about your mother? Why can't she inherit it? Isn't she in your father's will?"

Roscoe shrugged. "Sure. But she doesn't get the ranch. Father loves her—I guess, if he's capable of any emotion—but he doesn't think she or any woman can run a ranch. 'Ranching's man's work,' he always used to tell us when we were boys. And I guess he believes it."

"Be careful!" Burriss cautioned. "If you're caught, you won't get anything."

"Don't tell me what to do, Burriss. Leave it all to me."

The reverend sighed. "All right, Roscoe. Now what's this about some work?"

Roscoe launched into a vivid description, his eyes snapping.

Spur had just ground the cheroot into the dust with his boot heel when the two men left the house. Within a matter of moments they had ridden back to Main Street where they tied up in front of Peterson's.

McCoy watched the men enter the saloon, then ran down the street, got his mare from the sheriff's office and rode up and tied her near

160

the saloon. If he had to leave quickly he'd be ready.

Spur went into the bar. He scanned the room, searching every face. He couldn't see Roscoe Tate, but Parsons held up the bar with an elbow, his back to the door. The Secret Service agent looked to the stairs. Roxanna? Was Roscoe with her?

He walked to the stairs and ran up them without being seen by Parsons. Spur halted before Roxanna's door, then listened. No voices. Then a soft, sweet humming which occasionally broke into song issued from the room. Roxanna was probably alone, idling away her time. If so, where was Roscoe?

Spur decided he'd better duck into Roxanna's to see how she was, and to question her further concerning that cowboy who'd seen the three riders.

He knocked softly, the humming stopped abruptly, and a moment later the door opened, revealing Roxanna dressed in black silk stockings held up by a lacy, black garter belt. Her torso was tightly encased in a frilly black corset, above which her breasts lay bare, the nipples erect and rose-red. Roxanna smiled as Spur's gaze rose to her face.

"Hello," she said. "Mr. McCoy, I had you wrong. I didn't think you'd ever come back to me. I should have known you couldn't resist me." She laughed and moved back to allow him entrance, then closed the door and turned to him.

"Why don't we start by letting me undress you. Okay?" She smiled and walked to him, reaching out for his belt.

Spur didn't have time to respond or explain; a pounding knock echoed through the room.

"Roxanna!" a voice boomed outside.

"Roscoe?" he asked.

Roxanna nodded and started to speak, but Spur pushed his hand over her mouth. He put a finger to his lips, then looked around the room. The closet. He walked to it and opened the door. It was about eighteen inches wide and three feet long, stuffed with Roxanna's most intimate garments. Spur squeezed in between them. The last thing he saw before he closed the door was Roxanna's smiling face.

"Roxanna, damn it! Are you in there? Are you busy?"

"Yes and no," she said. "Come in!"

At that moment Spur opened the closet door slightly; he couldn't see Roxanna or Tate as he heard the other door swing open, but he had a clear view of the bed. The slips and petticoats, dresses and corsets pushing against him from all sides smelled of the familiar, sweet odor of woman mixed with perfumes and colognes of past times. Spur pushed it out of his mind. Roscoe must have been in a corner of the bar, or out the back, Spur thought. Perhaps in another room upstairs? Either way, he'd get a chance to eavesdrop on him. Maybe it would be useful.

"Ouch!" Roxanna said. "You're hurting me!"

"You know you love it, Roxanna!" Roscoe

growled and Spur heard the sound of ripping cloth. At that point Roxanna's musical laugh filled the room, blending with the man's rougher voice.

"You're paying for that," she said.

"That—and you."

Spur strained to see the pair but they were just out of his line of vision. He heard unstrapping and unbuckling, heavy garments tossed carelessly to the floor, and Roxanna's nearly constant giggles.

"See that big cock?" Roscoe's voice rasped. "It's going right up your cunt."

"I hope so," Roxanna said. "If you can keep it hard long enough."

"Bitch!" A moment later two naked bodies flashed by Spur's vision, then Roscoe pushed Roxanna onto the brass bed and fell heavily onto her.

His hairy body sharply constrasted with Roxanna's milky white, smooth skin. He lewdly ground his groin against hers, then bent to suck one of her ripe nipples. She arched her back and sighed, then threw her legs up until they gripped Roscoe around his deeply tanned back. Her ankles crossed.

"Stick it in me!" she said. "Right now!"

"Goddamn, Roxanna! You're the horniest woman I've ever met. I get a hard-on just hearing your name."

As Roxanna giggled Spur frowned. Say something important, dammit! Roscoe plunged into her, then vigorously pumped.

"I'll show them," Roscoe said between grunts. "Try to make a fool out of me! Nothing's going to stop me now."

"What?" Roxanna said, panting.

"Never mind. You don't need to talk now. Not with your mouth, at least."

Roscoe was silent for a moment after that, then sighed and thrust double-time, sending the bed into squeaks of complaint, bouncing its legs two inches off the floor.

"Oh yes!" Roxanna cried, her face flushed, mouth wide open. Her body slipped across the sheet as Roscoe sweated above her.

"Damn that bastard!" Roscoe said. "We'll show him. Tomorrow morning." The man gave a short, anguished cry as his body trembled, every muscle tensing as he unloaded into Roxanna.

Tomorrow morning? Spur frowned. What was Roscoe talking about? Was the *bastard* a farmer? Were *they* farmers in general?

Spur looked up to see Roscoe's shiny body lying motionless on top of Roxanna. His breath came in harsh gasps, his back pulsing with it.

Roxanna flailed her arms from side to side, trying to push the man away.

"Hey, Roscoe!" she said. "Would you roll off me, please? Jesus, you know how much you weigh! I'm such a fragile thing." She caressed his thighs and back and gently succeeded in slipping out from under the spent man. Roxanna lay back and wiped wisps of hair from her face.

"Whew, Roscoe! You sure know how to ride a woman!"

"Hell, Roxanna," he said, not moving. "You know I got the best cock in the county."

"That I do, Roscoe. Say, what was all that you were talking about? Sounds like you're upset about something—or more rightly, someone."

"What?" he asked groggily.

"You know, about *getting that bastard*, that kind of talk."

Roscoe sat up slowly, looked at the woman, then smiled. "Nothing. Just fucking out my problems, as usual." He reached out and touched her left breast.

"I see. Well, time's just about up. Would you like to pay me now, or later?"

"Shit. Now, I guess." He rose to his feet, stumbled across the floor and retrieved his pants. A moment later he produced a five dollar gold piece from a pocket and handed it to her.

Roxanna gasped. "Roscoe! Surely not all this?" She marveled at the coin.

"Sure. Plenty more where that comes from." He paused a moment, then dropped his pants and sat beside her on the bed. "Roxanna, I may be leaving here soon."

"Why?"

"Troubles. Family problems. You don't want to hear about that. But I wanted to talk to you about something."

Spur broke out in a sweat as the clothing pressed against him; the closet was close and hot.

"So talk," she said, reaching out to stroke his penis.

"Would you ever consider working somewhere else, some other town?"

"Leaving Kearney?" Roxanna's eyelashes fluttered in surprise. "Move to another town? I haven't really. Kearney's my home.'"

"Think about it."

She did, then cocked her head to one side saucily. "I might—if the price was right. I'd also have to be sure I was earning as much as I made here. What you got in mind?"

"Nothing yet. Just plans. But you wouldn't mind working in Denver, or St. Louis, or somewhere else, would you?"

"That depends on who I was working for."

"Keep your mind open, okay? Someday I may have a little surprise for you."

"I'll look forward to it, Roscoe." She gave him one last squeeze and released his organ. "Take good care of that for me, cowboy!"

Roscoe smiled and turned to dress. Roxanna playfully reached out and pinched his butt. "You're a fine figure of a man, Roscoe Tate. Generous too. Now if only you weren't such a damned bastard, you might make some woman very happy one day, I'm sure." But as she spoke she gazed at the gold piece.

Spur felt the sweat intensify, soaking his clothing. Why didn't Roscoe leave?

Roxanna laid the coin on a table before a large, expensive mirror. When she turned back Roscoe was buttoning up his fly.

"Thanks, Roxanna. You're a great woman."

"Come again anytime. And if I don't see you for a while—well, you know you're always welcome here."

"Thanks." He left.

Roxanna fell back onto the bed, sighing as she did so. Spur opened the closet door and stepped from the room, the sudden rush of air chilling his wet body.

"Some show, don't you think?" She laughed. "Some men pay big money to watch what you just got to watch for free. You're not the first man to hide in my closet. And you seemed to enjoy it—you're wetter than I am," she teased.

Spur stared down at her lovely naked body. "I think I've got all that I need. Thanks for letting me listen."

"Did it help you any? I mean, by listening in? I figured that's what you wanted to do."

"Maybe. I'll let you know." Spur left the room and gave his crotch a quick rub to check his growing erection. Tomorrow morning? Roscoe had big plans for the morning. McCoy headed down the hall and into the saloon. He just caught a glimpse of Roscoe and Parsons walking through the swinging doors onto Main Street.

Spur followed.

The men rode about three miles from Kearney, heading due west, Spur figured by the position of the sun. Spur hung back on the trip, hiding for a while behind a slow-moving hay wagon. Finally he saw the men turn onto a trail —above it was a sign with a capital P lying on its side. The lazy P. Parsons's ranch.

167

Spur turned back toward Kearney at a gentle walk. Something was going to happen tomorrow morning, he thought as he rode. If Roscoe had been partially responsible for the Parker murders, and maybe even organized the attack on the Craig's farm, he might be planning another for the morning. Sure, Spur thought. That fits. But where?

The Craig farm?

Spur decided it was a possibility. One more shot—do the job right this time. Go in, kill or scare out the Craigs. That's what Spur would do. The foiled attempt earlier that morning at the Craig's farm couldn't be allowed to pass into history; that would mean the ranchers had lost control of the homesteaders.

No. They had to complete their mission on the Craig farm. And if Roscoe was one of the men responsible, Spur thought, he'd be riding there early in the morning. Perhaps Parsons would ride with him.

And the third?

Spur shook his head. He knew one thing— he'd be at the Craig place before daybreak. Just in case.

CHAPTER SIXTEEN

"DON'T LET me catch you going out on the street again!" Rev. Burriss said, shaking his ever-present Bible with one hand at his daughter. He stood in the parlor of his comfortable Kearney home. "I'm going out now. I'll be gone about three hours, maybe longer. Just stay here and wait until I come back."

"Wait?" Ginny Burriss said, then laughed. "Wait for what? For you to come on back through that door yelling at me, telling me not to go outside, not to look at handsome men, not to have any damned fun!"

Burriss gave his daughter his sternest pulpit look. "I'll have no cursing in my house," he warned. "The Lord God shall punish thee, O wicked daughter! You are evil. This town's corrupted you, eaten away at your morals. And I won't let it corrupt you further. Stay here until I return!" he thundered.

Looking at her father, Ginny Burriss could

also see the black coat, vest, shirt, boots, and stovepipe hat her father always wore while preaching. As she continued to look at him, she was shocked at the changes she hadn't noticed earlier. Her father looked older; dark circles hung heavily beneath his eyes, and worry lines had furrowed across his face where once the skin had been taut. They'd lived in Kearney for three years and her father had not only turned into a tyrant—he had also grown old.

"Virginia Marilee Burriss, do you hear me?" he asked. "Sometimes I don't know what to do with you, girl. I should hand you over to Satan, for all the good I can do you."

Fatigue rocked through her brain and body. She was tired of his empty threats, tired of the insincere pleas for *getting herself washed in the blood of Jesus.* But she was also simply tired of her father. She knew she couldn't win against him.

"I'm sorry, Father," she said in her sweetest voice, a smile pasted onto unwilling lips. "I'll try harder to be a good child of God." She couldn't remove all traces of a sarcastic tone, but he didn't seem to notice.

Burriss flinched at the unexpected retreat, then frowned. "May He find thee in His favor." With that he stepped out the door.

Moments later Ginny heard the tumblers deep within the lock turn and fasten into place. She spun from the door and surpressed a scream. For months her father had grown increasingly fanatical in his words—but not his actions. Ginny had noticed that he had begun drinking more heavily, going out at all hours of the day and night, even swearing on occasion. Early one night, when her father had stumbled past her on the way to his bed she thought she smelled perfume on him—the expensive French type that some of the fancy women wore.

She sighed and didn't try to understand. She didn't want to understand. All she wanted was to have some man take her away from her father, to help her escape him. Ginny wanted to be her own wild, free self, not the starched, pure-white creature into which her father was trying to change her.

A man. Reverend Burriss had always taught his daughter that men were evil. She should never let them touch her, or return their gazes. And she certainly was never to do the *act of marriage*, as her father called it.

But she had. Several times. The last one was Spur McCoy. Ginny felt herself flush. A tingling spread out from her groin. Without thinking she reached for it, pressing both hands against her *v*, rubbing it gently through layers of petticoats and the stiff dress.

Ginny sat in the middle of the floor on the thick rug, her legs splayed far apart. She hiked up frilly cloth of various shades of pinks and pure whites, then worked her fingers between her legs and finally touched the furry patch. She groaned as she slipped one finger inside, moving it in and out, while another finger snaked up and began rubbing her clitoris.

Shock waves swept through her body as she rubbed herself. Ginny leaned back on one hand while her other one busied herself, her mouth forming an *o* as she shuddered through an orgasm.

She thought of Spur McCoy—his tanned, muscular body, his huge erection. Her fingers moved faster as she remembered his rough touch on her soft skin, how she knelt before him and he rammed his penis down her throat.

A series of cries and gasps issued from her throat as her hand became a blur between her legs, its caresses plunging her into paroxysms of delight and ecstasy.

There were others, too; other men, other times. Good times, she remembered, searching for a new fantasy, a new way to break the monotony, to quench her insatiable desire for sex. There was the cowboy who she'd bumped into one night when she was out looking for her father—the young man who'd opened his pants and showed her his hard penis in the moonlight, then put it in her.

Then there was Mr. Marshall, the general store owner, who'd closed early one afternoon and, after pulling down the window blinds, spread her out on the counter and took her in utter animal lust.

Ginny's body rocked with orgasms, her mind racing from scene to scene of her brief sexual life. Suddenly she stopped, almost gasping as the explosive action of her fingers ceased.

This was wrong, she told herself. Masturbation was evil, a tool of Satan to tempt the wicked. Her cheeks burned as she thought of the burning pools of Hell, of the Devil with his pitchfork, infernal fire, wailing sinners. Eternal damnation.

She should stop, she told herself. Stop, wipe your hands and pray to God that she never touched herself again. She should ask Jesus to cleanse her of wicked and evil thoughts.

Ginny Burriss sat for a moment, her hand frozen above her genitals, then shook her head. Her father was wrong. The Bible was wrong. It's wrong *not* to experience these delights, she told herself. That is what life's all about. Otherwise, God wouldn't have given us sex organs, she thought.

With this Ginny's hand pressed against herself again, hard. Her other rose to her breasts, squeezing the nipples, pinching them, cupping and rubbing the sensitive skin there.

She thought of every man who'd lain between her legs; the disgusting ones, the thrilling ones —and the feelings they'd aroused in her. Her hand was no match for a good, hard man, she thought briefly before all rationality was swept away on the crest of a wave of passion.

Her body shook as she fell back onto the rug, one hand jabbing violently at her crotch, the other squeezing her breasts alternately, while the sexual flush spread out across her face, neck and chest.

Ginny Burriss, wrapped in passion, didn't hear the tumblers within the lock rotate, nor the front door swing open. Two seconds later, however, she heard a loud intake of breath— shattering her passion, and forcing her head to look up at her father's incredulous face.

"Christ—shit—Ginny!" He didn't look into her eyes. "Slut! Whore! How dare you pleasure yourself on my best parlor rug! I'll kill you. I'll kill you now and let the Lord take charge of your soul. That's all I can do now!" he said threateningly. Burriss swung the door closed without taking his gaze off her body.

Ginny was too stunned to move for several seconds. Then she removed her hands, straightened her skirts, and started to rise. Only then did she notice that, although she'd covered up her body, her father's eyes continued to rest on her crotch. He hadn't stopped looking there since he'd walked into the room, surprising her.

"I won't say I'm sorry, Father," she said. "This isn't the first time. I do this every day, sometimes several times a day. When you go out, when you lock me in my room, or when you're asleep at night."

"Abomination!" He looked up at her face, finally.

"And it feels good."

"Heathen slut!"

"What did you expect me to do? Sit quietly in the corner, hands folded, waiting for your return? You never let me go to the dances with the local men. When one comes to call on me, you tell them I'm not home. Since I couldn't have many men, I pretended I had one."

"Ginny!" her father said.

"Why don't you try it, Daddy?" Ginny said viciously. "Or do you already do it? Do you feel yourself at night, Daddy?"

Rage prevented Burriss from speaking. He took two halting steps toward his daughter.

"I'll bet you do," Ginny said, sneering. She faced her father fearlessly. All her hesitation, her weariness of her father vanished. Maybe she didn't need a man to break off from her father. Maybe she could do it on her own. She was nearly nineteen—plenty old enough to be free, to do what she pleased. "I'll bet you pull your thing every day, Daddy! And then pray to God afterwards to forgive you for being such a lowly sinner. Or do you, Father? Do you really pray—have you ever really prayed—or are you acting all the time?"

"Filthy slut!" Burriss slammed his hand down hard against Ginny's face, knocking her to the floor. She crumpled and screamed. "I'll teach you to speak to a man of the cloth that way!"

"You're no preacher, Father. And you're sure no Christian!" Ginny rubbed her cheek, trying to stamp out the pain. "You drink and swear and lay with Roxanna Stafford—don't think I don't know what you do when you go out!"

He stared at her in astonishment for a moment, then smiled evilly. Ginny looked at him in horror as she rose. Then she saw the distortion at his crotch—the way the material bulged out at the front of his pants. Her father was aroused. Her father—

"So you want a man inside you, do you?" her father asked, throwing all pretensions of Christianity away. Ginny had never seen her father this way. "Isn't that why you do such things?"

"Stay away from me," she said, pushing her hands out before her, but fear clutched her throat. She felt behind her—the wall. If she could make it to her room she could wait until he cooled off.

"You want a man? Huh? Well, daughter, you're damned well going to get one. Little lady, I'll make you see God. Or the devil, in this case."

"No!" she cried. "Father! It's a sin! That's what you taught me, remember?"

"What the hell do you care about sin? Or me, for that matter? Come on, Ginny. You know you want it. Any cock'll do, isn't that it?"

"No!" She bolted to the right, but her father easily caught her.

"Stay right there, little lady." He grasped one of her hands in his, and after pressing his knees against hers to hold her body in place, he lowered her hand to his crotch, then pushed it hard against him. "Feel that?"

Ginny held back the urge to vomit, then cried out in rage and disgust. She kicked her father's shins but he didn't seem to notice the blows. His evil face, inches from her, shot out hot breath that struck her like poisonous fumes. Gathering every ounce of energy she jabbed her fingers savagely against the man's erection, then repeated the motion and pulled her hand free as Burriss moved his hand to cup and protect the area.

"Shit! Jesus Christ!" Burriss yelled, bent over at the waist, one hand rubbing his damaged genitals. "You've nearly unmanned me, wicked girl!"

"Feel that, Father?" she said. Ginny turned and ran into her father's room, then slammed the door shut and locked it. Feeling calm, as if she wasn't participating in the action but merely observing another moving about on a stage, Ginny Burriss shoved a chair up beneath the doorknob and then walked to the window. She was glad she'd run into her father's room—her bedroom had been specially designed without windows.

Ginny pulled the curtains back, slid the window open, hiked up her skirt and petticoats, and stuck one booted foot out the window. With a bit of straining and stretching she was soon outside.

Her pulse pounded in her ears and before her eyes as she walked, then broke into a run. She turned down Main Street and headed toward Sheriff Gardner's office. He should know what to do. Surely he wouldn't side with her father. Then she stopped. No. The questions, the trial, the looks of her neighbors. She couldn't do it, couldn't go through the shame. Desperation clouded her thoughts; she turned to the right, then the left, stumbling over her feet, her hands hanging limply at her sides, not knowing where to turn, and the scream she'd earlier choked down tore from her throat as she fell to the dusty road.

CHAPTER SEVENTEEN

SHOULD I tell Gardner? Spur wondered as he stopped the horse in its tracks, one hundred feet from the sheriff's combination office and jail. Spur paused for a moment; he didn't have proof that Roscoe Tate was responsible for the Parker murders, nor that he and Jack Parsons were planning on striking the Craig farm in the morning. But it made sense, fit the facts, and it was the most that Spur had to go on.

Spur began moving the horse toward the sheriff's office again. As he passed an alley he heard the sound of approaching feet—then watched as a young woman collapsed onto the street, screaming.

"Hey!" he called, springing off the horse and running to her. He recognized Ginny Burriss. "Ginny! What's wrong?" He reached down and helped her to her feet, but it was a few seconds before she opened her eyes and allowed Spur to touch her again.

"Are you all right?" he asked as she rubbed her eyes and looked around her. She blushed slightly.

"I must look a mess."

"You look fine, Ginny."

"I'm sorry." She lowered her head for a moment, then stared up at him earnestly. "I was afraid, and I was just running anywhere—and then everything seemed to close in on me—and that's all I remember."

"Why were you running?"

"To get away from my father."

"What's he done now?" Spur asked, remembering the scene her father had made in his hotel room.

"He—he—he's chasing me. I hurt him." Ginny shook her head. "No. I can't tell you any more. It's too awful." With those words she collapsed into his arms and shook as she cried.

"Ginny, I'm sure you have nothing to worry about," he said softly as he stroked her hair. "If your father's after you, we'd better get off the streets."

"Please!" she said between sobs. "I don't want him to find me. I never want to see him again!"

"Then you don't have to."

She stopped crying, sniffling a few times, and wiped away the moisture from her cheeks. "Okay."

Spur could see the woman was deeply troubled by something, but it was obvious he wasn't going to learn what that was—not now, at least.

He took the horse's reins in one hand, put an arm around her shoulder and started off toward the Calico Hotel, but Ginny violently tore away from the contact.

"No! Don't touch me. If he sees me—or if anyone sees you touching me—he'll explode!" Her eyes were wild.

Spur raised his hands in defeat, then dropped them to his sides. A strange girl, he thought. Her father had turned the young, vibrant, sensual woman of a few days ago into a blubbering, timid mouse. What could have happened to her that had done that?

"You're not going back home?"

She didn't look at him as she shook her head violently. "Never. Not when he's there. I'll wait until he's gone—maybe Sunday morning when he's preaching—and then go in and get all my things. I'll put all my money together and go somewhere where he'll never find me."

"How will you live? Your money won't last very long. What about after that?"

"There are ways—for a woman to make money," she said slowly.

"Ginny," Spur began.

She shot him a look and stopped walking. "Why the hell not? My father already thinks I'm a whore. Why shouldn't I go ahead and become one? If only for a while, until I save up enough to live on?" She laughed bitterly. "I'd hate to disappoint him."

"We'll talk about this later," Spur said, glancing at several men and a pair of women who'd looked toward them, attracted by

181

Ginny's loud voice.

They walked to the hotel in silence, the horse accompanying them.

Once inside Spur's room, Ginny splashed water on her face, bending over the basin. Spur admired her fine backside then, remembering how exciting and bold she'd been in bed. She'd had none of the maidenly reserve that too many women maintained, even while rocking through orgasm after orgasm. Spur had enjoyed her immensely.

"What happened at your father's house?" Spur asked when the woman had finished patting her face dry. Where a few moments ago there had been redness or puffiness, her face was now freshly pink, glowing, radiating beauty.

"It's too awful," she said. "I don't want to talk about it. I can't think how I'd tell you. It's—beastly."

"Try me," Spur said. "After what we've done, we're at least good friends by now."

She smiled once—and her face lit up. She sniffled again and sat in the straight back chair that was pushed up near Spur's bed, then lay her hands in her lap and folded them.

"Well, he'd just gone out," she said with perfect calm and dignity. "I was in the middle of the parlor, and suddenly I thought of when I'd snuck in here and surprised you, and then had fun together." She looked down at her hands. "That was one of the best times I've ever had, Spur, in my whole life! And sometimes when I think of things like that, I just have to touch myself there, feel myself, reliving the moment. You know what I mean?"

"Go on," Spur said.

"Well, I was in the middle of the parlor doing that—and my father walked in! I thought he would kill me, at first—he was so furious at me doing such a wicked thing. That's what he said, at least. But after a while it seemed like he was more than angry—and—and I saw he was getting excited. He wanted to lay with me, like men and women do! Spur, I didn't know what to think, what to say. Ever since we came to Kearney he's been a wicked man. He used to be gentle, a true Christian in every sense of the word. Now he's become a different person. He goes out at all hours of the night, sometimes early in the morning, before the sun's up."

Spur's brain latched onto that piece of information, but he didn't interrupt Ginny's narration.

"So I told him it was a sin, but he didn't care, and thought I didn't either. And he—he made me touch his hard—well, you know. His man thing." She squirmed. "I wanted to retch; I felt myself getting sick. So I jabbed him hard in the crotch, twice, and ran for the closest room. I locked the door, pushed a chair under the knob, and climbed out the window. I was just running from the house when I collapsed in the street."

"I see," Spur said. "You jabbed him in the groin?"

"Yes. I didn't know what else to do—and I was afraid imagining what he might make me do if I didn't stop him."

"You're a very resourceful girl," he said.

She stiffened her back and composed her face. "I'm a young lady," she thought for a moment. "Well, a young woman. Maybe not a lady anymore."

"My apologies," Spur said. "Any fool could see you're a young lady!"

"So I'm leaving Kearney and never want to see my father again," she said suddenly, as if to test the plan's reality.

"Are you going to the sheriff's office? You could have your father arrested."

"I—I don't know. I'm not sure I want to go through all that—and if I told Gardner I know I'd have to see my father again, go to trial—" She sighed. "I just want to collect a few things and leave." She stood then, and kissed him lushly on the lips. "Thanks."

"For what?"

"If I hadn't remembered the time we did it, my father wouldn't have caught me playing with myself, and I wouldn't be breaking free from him right now."

"I see," Spur said. "Do you have any immediate plans?"

"What do you mean?"

"If you want, you can stay here for a while—a few days, if you wish. Until you can get the things you want."

"That would be wonderful!" she cried, clasping his shoulders, her hands traveling down to his biceps, where she couldn't possibly touch her thumb to her fingertips while they were wrapped around his powerful muscles. "And maybe we could do it again—sometime soon? Not now, but maybe later?"

"Of course."

"But if I'd be in the way—I wouldn't want to put you out. If you have a different girl in here every night, I can find somewhere else to stay."

McCoy smiled. "No need."

She relaxed then. "Wonderful. Do you have anything to do right now?"

"Yes. I was on my way to Sheriff Gardner's office."

"Why?"

Spur smiled shortly. "Business."

"I see. I'm sure I can find something to do."

"Keep the door locked, if you want. And if you go out—"

"I'll be careful," Ginny said, shivering. "I don't want to give my father the chance."

"Fine."

She raised herself up on her toes, lifting her face at the same time.

It was the most obvious kiss proposal Spur had ever seen. He leaned down and their lips touched. Spur's tongue probed, broke through the sensuous lips, and slipped into her hot mouth. He pulled her to him then, pushing his crotch against her body, feeling her erecting nipples jabbing his chest. His penis had throbbed to full erection by the time the kiss ended, and it was with an effort that Spur pulled himself back from the woman.

"Goodbye, Ginny."

"Bye."

Spur left the room.

Sheriff Gardner snorted. "Where's your evidence?" he demanded of the man standing on the other side of his desk. "You don't have one single shred of evidence, Spur."

"I'll admit that, Gardner, but it's the—"

"And there's a big hole in your little scheme. According to your sources three men attacked the Parker place, right?"

"Yes," Spur said, standing across the desk.

"Roscoe and Parsons are only two. Who's the third?"

"I don't know."

Gardner nodded and gave a short chuckle. "I'm sorry I got so riled up there, but that's just the kind of thing that I was thinking about two weeks ago."

"Why didn't you move, then?" Spur asked.

"No evidence. Couldn't do a thing. I had ideas —but that's all."

"You suspected Roscoe Tate and Jack Parsons?" Spur asked.

Gardner paused, nodded, then shook his head. "Yes. Well, no. Maybe not those two particular men. I suspected all of them, but I never had the chance to prove my suspicions."

Spur slid into the chair before the desk and faced Gardner. "That's what we can do now— tomorrow morning. I'll ride out there and if no one shows, I'll know I was wrong. If some men do show with thoughts of trouble, I'll know I was at least partly right. And if Roscoe Tate and Jack Parsons arrive there around dawn—with a third man—and attack the Craig farm . . ."

"Okay, okay," Gardner said. "Go ahead. Do it."

Spur smiled. "I wasn't asking for your permission. I have jurisdiction over you here. I simply wanted your opinion."

"Sounds good to me," he said slowly, "although a long shot."

"I'll let you know what happens." Spur began to rise from the chair.

"Hold on, Spur! It could be too dangerous for one man. I know you think you can do it alone—and you did once, I'll give you that. But you won't get lucky again. It just makes more sense to have more than one man there—in case your fears prove real."

Spur nodded. "Maybe. But I like to work alone."

"So how about me and some men going out there to back you up?"

Spur looked hard at the man. "If you can keep them back, well out of sight."

Gardner nodded. "I'll round up the men quietly, only the ones I trust the most. Then we'll ride out of town at different times, heading different directions, but meet at the Craig place—some time late tonight, early in the morning. And you?"

Spur shrugged. "Probably the same." The thought of all those extra men made him uneasy. The raiding party could discover them and change plans—and Spur might never find out who killed the Parkers. But the backups might come in handy, Spur conceded, if they were secreted correctly.

"You know, if you're sure it's Roscoe Tate and Jack Parsons—"

"Which I'm not," Spur butted in.

"—you could follow them tonight, or even watch their ranches."

"Could," Spur said, musing over the idea.

"Don't worry about my men," Gardner said. "They won't get in the way unless they have to." He shook his head. "I hope you're right—and I hope this puts an end to the problems here in the Platte River Valley."

"My sentiments exactly," Spur said.

"But I've got doubts. Still—" he shook his head. "Any other news to bother me with? How's the investigation into the Fred Lucas killing coming along?"

"I was going to ask you the same thing," Spur said. "I've been concentrating on the Parkers."

"I haven't had any luck on it, either," Gardner said. "I've tried."

"I've also got a little story to tell you."

Gardner looked at him in surprise. "Story?"

Spur launched into a description of the trouble between Burriss and his daughter Ginny. He didn't leave much to the imagination. When he was finished Gardner was grim.

"I knew Burriss had gone bad, running around and causing some trouble, but I had no idea he was capable of trying to commit incest. The man's changed. How's Ginny taking it?"

"As well as can be expected."

"Why didn't she come to me?"

"She didn't want to cause any trouble, and she wants to leave Kearney as quickly and quietly as she can. Could you arrest her father —and get a conviction—without her help?"

"Don't know," Gardner said, scratching his head. "But I know Burriss won't be welcome in Kearney for much longer. If I can't use the law to force him out—I'm sure the citizens around here will do the trick." He smiled ruefully. "He's not the first *preacher* to be run out of town."

"I'm beginning to wonder about Rev. Burriss. He doesn't sound much like a Bible man. Ginny described what he's been doing lately—and I don't like the picture she painted."

"Burriss has gone bad; no one will deny that. Still, he's the only preacher we've got and people keep on going to church every Sunday to hear him preach." He laughed. "Every Sunday we hear him ask God to forgive our sins, and his as well. Maybe he thinks that makes him pure."

"Wouldn't know."

"I'll set out rounding up the men. If not before, I'll see you at daybreak at Craig's?"

"Probably," Spur said. "I just might follow one of the men after all, as you suggested. Let's wait until two hours after sunrise to call it quits. If they haven't shown by then, I was wrong."

"Sure," Gardner said, then laughed. "You're the boss."

CHAPTER EIGHTEEN

SPUR STRETCHED out a leg to loosen the stiff muscles, then tucked it back under him. He'd been crouched over in a shadow in front of the Lazy P ranch for nearly three hours. No sleep for him tonight, he thought ruefully. He was sure it would be worth it. And he'd had worse experiences.

After leaving Gardner's office, Spur had ridden back to Jack Parsons's ranch. He moved carefully toward the house—both horses stood there where they'd been left hours earlier. Both Parsons and Tate, then, were still inside.

Spur spent the time thinking, going over and over the facts, to see if his conclusions were correct. No matter how many times he did this, Spur McCoy always had the same result: Roscoe and Parsons and another man had killed the Parkers, or were involved in the killings, if they hired other men—and that they were going

191

to attempt the same thing with the Craigs on the coming morning.

He was sure Gardner and his men were in position by then, or soon would be. Spur hoped that they damn well wouldn't get in his way. He disliked the idea of their presence—hell, he was sorry he'd told Sheriff Gardner his thoughts in the first place. But the backup men could come in handy, if things didn't happen according to plan.

He looked around him with a start when the faint sound of a horse and rider tattooed itself into his brain. It approached from directly before him, where the trail to Kearney stood out clearly in the moonlight. Spur, realizing he might be seen by someone approaching from that direction, moved further into the shadows, and then ducked around behind a bush.

A few minutes later Spur could see who was riding up to the Lazy P. A big man—a light-colored hat—but Spur couldn't see the man's face, not even when he passed within twenty feet of him. He frowned. Who'd be riding out to Jack Parsons's ranch at this hour of the early morning?

The third man? The one who'd helped them kill the Parkers?

Spur grunted, then ran forward to follow the man. The unknown rider dismounted and tied the horse up before the farmhouse, then walked directly in without knocking or pausing, as if expected.

Spur moved back to his shadowy corner near

the gate and frowned. It was a long wait to day-break. Should he ride out to Craig's place now, or wait to see if the men leave? Spur decided to stay put; he just had a *feeling* about Roscoe Tate.

He pulled the coat tighter around him and leaned back, relaxing into the position.

Spur was startled out of a light sleep by the slap of moisture on his face. His Stetson had fallen back against the tree trunk he'd been leaning against, squatting on his toes. The droplet bolted him into a standing position. He pushed the hat forward onto his head.

Night. He must have dozed off for a couple minutes, no more. Raindrops fell heavily around him, sending up splashes of dust as the liquid hit the dry-as-bones Nebraska soil. Spur raised his face into it for a few stinging seconds to wake him fully, then turned to examine the surrounding area. The sun hadn't yet streaked the eastern sky with its first colors.

A door banged shut somewhere far away, causing a dog to bark. "Shit," Spur muttered. The rain stopped. He saw the three men move to their horses in the distance. They swiftly mounted and rode directly toward Spur and the gate. He ducked back away from the trail and moved quickly toward his horse.

He didn't want to miss any of the action he knew would be coming at the Craig farm.

Spur didn't bother waiting for the men to catch up with him; nor did he decide to follow them at a distance, to make sure they were headed for the Craig farm. He didn't think they were.

He *knew* so.

Spur cut across the completely flat land for several miles. His mount's eyes were clear and good, for she avoided all obstructions even in the moonlight. He saved time by not following established trails and roads that had been etched into the plains by centuries of use— long before any ranchers or farmers had settled the area.

His horse tired and began to falter on the last mile, so Spur slowed her to a walk.

"'Good girl," he said, rubbing her neck. "Not too much farther." If he was reading the stars right he was moving in the correct direction.

As he approached the Craig farm deep purple tinted the east, showing gathering storm clouds. Dawn was approaching.

He moved his horse into a thicket of hickory trees, tied her up, rubbed her down for ten minutes, keeping his eyes alert. He stood about a hundred feet from the gate which led into the Craig farm itself. Spur crossed the ground quickly, looking for a place to hide until the men showed—which could be at any second. Sure enough, as he ran toward the henhouse full of clucking chickens and a vociferous rooster, Spur heard the men's horses moving quickly toward him. He had just made it inside the henhouse when the three men discreetly slowed their horses to a walk, then finally dismounted, walking beside them.

"Damned sure of themselves, aren't they?" Spur said to himself. As they grew closer Spur could see the kerchiefs wrapped around the men's lower faces. No way to identify them—although one of the hats looked exactly like one he'd seen perched on Roscoe's head recently. He was sure the men were Roscoe, Parsons and one other.

The men had apparently decided on a different approach than the one they'd used here last at Craig's—or rather, their hired men had used. As a rooster pecked at his boot Spur scanned the area visible between the door and jamb as the men broke up—one larger man moving to the rear of the farmhouse, the other two evenly dividing up the property between them. The two in front—the only ones Spur could see—stood about sixty feet from the house.

Now, Spur's nerves screamed. Raise your Spencer and blow the two men to hell, before they can hurt Julius Craig or his daughter Leah. Spur had to fight the urge to open fire on the men. He had to do this in accordance with the law—by the book. Especially when the sheriff was watching. Spur wondered where his men had hidden—he didn't see any sign of them. Gardner must have done a good job.

The two men stood motionless for a few moments, then one raised his rifle toward the kitchen window. Before the man could shoot the sharp, crackling explosion of a discharging rifle ripped through the early morning quiet, from behind the raiders, to their right, from a clump of trees.

The chickens broke into a new chorus of cackles as Spur watched out the door. The two men immediately ducked and ran for cover; Spur glanced at the area from which the shot had originated, silently cursing the man who'd fired early. Spur aimed two shots toward an overturned table behind which one of the men had ducked. Both men had apparently been spared from the trigger-happy idiot. Now Spur almost wished he'd been the one to shoot the early round—at least one of the men would be nothing but dead meat by now.

Hot .44 slugs flew through the air towards him as the two men bombarded the entire area. They occasionally shot toward the henhouse but concentrated most of their fire toward the clump of trees. Spur saw a flicker of movement in the corner of his eye; then turned and aimed. A man near the house ducked out of sight before Spur could fire. He was the third man, coming to the front to help out the other two, or was he pushed there by gunfire?

Spur couldn't tell how many men were shooting all around him, but he was convinced he'd never seen so many lousy shots in one place, from one group of men, in his life. After a few seconds Spur heard the farmhouse windows shattering, then someone shooting from within the house. Good, Spur thought. The Craigs were fighting back.

McCoy finally saw his victim. It was the second when a target and weapon line up and the moment seems frozen in time, and he held his breath until the connection between life and death had been made.

One of the men rose from his hiding place and ran across the yard, apparently in an attempt to remove himself from the fight. Spur blasted two rounds at him, leading him perfectly. The head and shoulders shook, the arms were thrown up and the figure wobbled grotesquely, spasming as it fell to the earth backwards. It lay motionless.

One down.

As Spur calmly surveyed the area, fresh from his first blood of the fight, he saw too late the figure of a man rapidly leaving the area on horseback. The man turned back for a second in fear—and Spur clearly saw the face. It was the fallen minister, Burriss!

McCoy cursed the man as he fired at what was apparently the only other man there. He wondered if it was Roscoe or Parsons.

Dawn threw riotous colors over the area where the clouds had broken up, charging it and the earth with an incredibly vivid crimson light. It cast a surreal feel to the otherwise earthy scene of carnage.

Spur kept firing at the hidden figure, but the man didn't make a mistake—didn't show himself too long, or even on the same side of the obstruction twice in succession. Spur wondered how long the man could hold out.

When he realized that the man hadn't returned fire for a minute or so, he stood tensely for a few seconds, then abruptly whistled. The shooting, which had been sporadic at best, stopped around him. He ducked back down and waited a moment. The man didn't fire. Was he dead, unconscious, out of ammunition—or crafty?

"Come out of there," Spur called out. "Show yourself. You can't possibly save yourself now. Your friends are dead, and you'll join them in two seconds if you don't get your butt out where I can see you."

"Fuck you!" the voice said, shaky but strong and deep. Spur recognized the voice instantly.

"Come on, Roscoe!" he yelled. "Let's talk this thing over. Cooperate with me, and I'll let you off easily."

"Not a chance, asshole! Goddamn it, I should've had you killed when I had the chance! I was right about you! You're nothing but trouble. Why don't you go back where you came from and leave me alone!"

"Too late for that. Let's talk."

"Fuck you," the man repeated.

Spur waited a moment, then lightly moved out over the rough ground as the rain started again. The sky spat out a drenching downpour toward the parched earth, which effectively muffled the sounds of Spur's movements as he approached the upturned table. When he was ten feet from it, he bent at the waist and scrambled up to it, then sprang up to his full height before it, aiming down behind the table.

Empty.

The man was gone.

Spur swore as he looked around—and just

caught a pair of feet disappearing around the back of the house.

He ran after Roscoe as the rain continued to pound down. The man couldn't have gone too far—Spur rounded the house and again caught the sight of the departing Roscoe darting around the other side, splashing in the instant puddles.

This is absurd, he thought, and abruptly turned, then ran the opposite direction, stopped, and aimed chest-level at nothing.

As quickly as it had started the rain stopped. Roscoe appeared before him, his head turned back to glance behind.

"Looking for me?" Spur asked.

Roscoe jerked his head and glanced wildly up at him. The mask was half-torn from his face, revealing enough for Spur to firmly identify him. Roscoe's hands were empty.

"Shit!" Roscoe said, then started to move.

"No," Spur said sharply. "Don't run. If you so much as spit I'll scramble your brains with hot lead."

Roscoe stood motionless.

It was only then that Spur saw the small stains on the man's clothing—one on his right thigh, another in his left shoulder. The rain had smeared them into long streaks.

"Tell me about the Parkers," Spur said.

"Fuck you. Why the hell should I tell you anything? You're not the sheriff."

Spur lowered his aim slightly. "If you say one more word without answering my question I'll blow your balls off."

The man's throat tightened visibly as he stared at the Spencer aimed at his crotch. He nodded.

"Yeah. Fuck yes I rode out to the Parkers the other week! Me and Burriss and Parsons. But look at you!" he said, sneering. "You and those men out there watching us. You killed Burriss and Parsons. How's that different from what happened to the Parkers? That was an accident."

Spur laughed. "Accident?"

"I swear it's the truth!"

"Bullshit. You killed those three people. Why?"

"Because—hell, because I hated old man Parker and I wanted all the homesteaders out of Kearney. We set fire to their house, yes, to warn the other farmers."

"And you shot and killed Al Parker?" Spur asked, guessing.

"That's right." Roscoe rubbed his shoulder. "I'm shot," he said.

Spur ignored him. "Why did you want the homesteaders out of Kearney County? You're no rancher; your family told me that. And you don't seem to be the type to stick around this cowtown. What's your scheme? Waiting around for your father to die for your inheritance?"

"I wanted to clear out the homesteaders so they wouldn't interfere with the Circle T. It was on its way to becoming the biggest outfit in the area. I figured as soon as it was going as well as it ever would, I'd take as much money as I could and leave here forever."

"And do what?" Spur asked.

"Maybe open a saloon; I don't know." The man grimaced as he touched his shoulder.

"You hired those three men to come here yesterday morning to kill the Craigs?"

"No! Not to kill them," he said. "Just to warn them to leave here." He looked up at Spur in disgust. "I suppose it was you who killed them," he said accusingly.

"Damn right! That's my job. They were threatening the Craigs. Anything else you want to confess before I turn you over to Sheriff Gardner?"

"No," Roscoe said, then bent at the waist as it pained. He fell to the wet ground.

Spur stood still. "Roscoe?"

The man lay motionless.

"Roscoe?"

His face was half-pressed into the muddy ground. Spur saw the man's hand flash into action, then the glint of steel. He aimed and fired before Roscoe could raise the hidden derringer from his boot. The round ripped through Roscoe's chest, slamming him back to the ground. His head rolled at a strange angle, the eyes glazed and lifeless, unblinking as massive droplets of water hit them and slid off.

Spur sighed. He walked warily to the corpse and, after pushing it several times and looking at the man's eyes, decided that Roscoe Tate was officially dead.

CHAPTER NINETEEN

Two BODIES. Spur looked at the downed men as he walked to the farmhouse. Sheriff Gardner limped out from the front door of the house and greeted Spur halfway. The rain had stopped, and the wind had split the clouds and pushed them away. A deep blue sky shone overhead.

"Come on out, you men," Gardner called.

From various strategic locales around the farm ten men appeared.

"You were right," Gardner said. "Obviously. It was Roscoe Tate all the time."

"You all right, Sheriff?" Spur asked as the two men stopped three feet from each other, the posse gathering around them.

"Sure. Just fell and hurt my leg in there, dammit! I'm fine." He looked at his men. "But I'm not so sure about these guys. Which one of you men fired early?"

He stared hard at the group; no one said a word.

Spur looked at the men curiously. They were farmers, to a man, which may have accounted for their lack of expertise at handling firearms. Men from Ohio and Pennsylvania aren't necessarily the best shots.

"Come on," Gardner said. "Tell me. No use trying to hide it. I'll find out soon enough."

"I've got to go," Spur said.

"What's that?"

"Burriss left—he was the one who rode out. I've got to follow him and bring him in."

"Right," Gardner said. "Go ahead. I'll finish up here."

"Spur!" a musical voice called out.

He glanced toward the farmhouse where Leah Craig stood in the doorway. She ran to him, wrapped her arms around him and pressed her face against Spur's chest.

"I worried about you out here!" she said, then pulled away from him. "I mean, I'm so glad you're safe. Thank you for saving my life again."

"My pleasure, Leah."

"Not now," Julius Craig said from the house as he appeared in the doorway behind his daughter. "He's got to get on and grab the good reverend before he slips out of town." The man grimaced as he touched a freshly-bandaged thigh. Leah had apparently ripped away the trouser leg and dressed the wound herself.

"You hurt bad, Craig?" Spur asked.

"I'll live."

"Get out of here, Spur," Gardner said, then smiled. "Thanks for your help."

"Sure," Spur said, then broke into a trot through the mud toward his horse. As the goo slapped against his boots Spur tried to forget how good Leah Craig had smelled, pressed up against him.

Rev. Edward Burriss hurriedly unlocked his front door, pushed it open, and slammed the key back into the lock as he closed it. He ran to his bedroom where he extracted a thick leather wallet from behind a picture. He glanced inside it—the neat stacks of hundred dollar bills were in place. He was glad he'd changed the church funds into these convenient bills last week. Those *donations* from Roscoe Tate sure had beefed up the coffers.

Burriss threw the money into a saddle bag, then added a shaving mug, brush, soap and comb. He looked at the large Bible lying on a table near the fireplace. He turned from it, then sighed.

"Shit."

He went to it and picked it up, then stuffed it into the bag. It might come in handy soon. He might have to pose as a preacher. Again.

Burriss couldn't believe his incredible luck in escaping the Craig farm that morning. And he hadn't been followed on his way back. He hoped both Roscoe and Parsons had been killed, thereby silencing them forever about his involvement with Roscoe's crimes.

Of course, he couldn't count on this, so he decided to leave Kearney. No sense in hanging around waiting for trouble.

He didn't flinch at the thought of his two partners lying dead on the muddy ground back there. They had been necessary evils. Now that he'd given up all pretenses to following that stifling, dull, stupid religion he could put up with some small problems—especially when he saw the possible money to be made.

Burriss shut the saddle bag, pulled the straps tight and hefted it. He pulled his pocket watch out—five till ten. The next train came through at 10:30. With luck he'd be far gone from Kearney by noon.

Where should he go? Burriss snorted as he gripped the bag and walked toward the door. He didn't care where. As long as he could hide out and—

Burriss looked at Ginny's bedroom door.

Ginny. He'd forgotten Ginny. Was she there? A quick check of her room ruled that out. Ginny, his pride and joy—no, his disappointment, he remembered bitterly. The girl was a slut, and she certainly wasn't his daughter any more. He pushed his feelings for her aside and hardened his face. Edward Burriss had no reason to stay in Kearney. Not any more.

He moved to the door, turned to survey the house, knowing this was the last time he'd do so, then reached for the knob.

Spur saw no signs of Burriss, but the man had headed west—probably toward Kearney. Trusting his instincts, Spur nudged the horse in that direction.

She was rested, frisky in the cool morning air.

Spur pushed her as much as he could, trying to figure out what Burriss was doing. Probably leaving town.

Too bad Gardner hadn't already arrested Burriss—then he would have been out of the way. But the sheriff had said there were some problems with that—Ginny not wanting to testify. Too late now.

Spur pulled up in back of Burriss's home. An exhausted horse stood there, sniffing the greenish water in the trough. Burriss must have just arrived.

He tied up the horse, walked to the front of the house, moved onto the porch and reached for the knob. It began to turn before he gripped it, so Spur laid himself flat on the wall next to the door's hinges. It swung open, halted a moment, then moved back.

Spur was ready as Burriss appeared from behind the door. McCoy knocked the man backward with a hard fist to the jaw, then pounded twice into his gut. He sprang back, light on his feet, feeling the glow of satisfaction from beating Burriss. A bag skidded across the porch where the reverened threw it.

"Going somewhere?" Spur asked.

"You're—the man with Ginny! What the hell concern is it of yours whether I'm going somewhere or not?" Burriss' face contorted with pain.

"Kearney doesn't let murderers leave town," Spur said. "Or men who try to sleep with their daughters."

Burriss backed away, stumbling when he

stepped off the porch backwards onto the walkway leading to the street. "Leave me alone. I don't know what you're talking about. I'm a man of God."

Spur laughed. "Gardner and I both heard Roscoe Tate say you were the third man in the Parker killings," Spur said with satisfaction. "He told us just before he died."

"He's crazy," Burriss said, sweating. "He named me at random. I haven't done anything wrong. Roscoe's just mad at me because I won't let him marry Ginny."

"I saw you this morning at Craig's. Let's go."

"Where to?" Burriss asked, rubbing his stomach.

"Jail. We usually hang men who kill women and children."

Burriss moved to the right, but Spur stuck out his foot and caught it under the man's legs, sending him sprawling to the ground. As Burriss looked up he saw Spur's Colt .45 out and ready.

"Don't try that again," Spur said.

"None of it's true! It's all lies!" Burriss said, real fear tinging his words.

"The Parkers. Two weeks ago. You were one of the three men. You helped kill the Parkers. Admit it!" Spur said.

"No." Burriss shook his head, his eyes wide open. "I—" He finally looked down. "I didn't want to. I found out what he was planning to do, and faced Roscoe. He gave a very generous donation to the church and said there was more if I joined him. He also threatened me—said if I didn't agree to do whatever he said he'd kill me. What else could I do?"

"Told Gardner, had Roscoe locked up. If you had the Parkers would be alive today. Come on, Burriss. You're a cold-blooded killer out to get as much money as you can, no matter what stands in the way."

At the mention of money Burriss glanced over to the fallen saddlebag on the porch. Spur followed the man's gaze, then carefully walked to the porch, keeping his eyes toward Burriss. He reached behind him with his left hand and pulled the bag off the porch.

"What's this?" Spur asked.

Burriss looked defeated. Spur felt inside the bag and soon found what he was hunting for.

"Where'd you get all this money, preacher?" Spur asked as he brought out the bills. "There must be four, five thousand here. Religion's a good business, wouldn't you say? I'm sure the church could use this. Maybe they'll hire a real preacher next time."

Spur slung the bag over his shoulder and pulled the man to his feet, then walked him to Main Street, then down it to the sheriff's office, his Colt pressed against the man's spine.

Several men and women looked at them as they walked down Main Street, but none said a word. Few faces seemed surprised at the spectacle of their preacher being taken to jail.

Once there, Spur again saw the blank-faced

boy sitting behind the desk. This time he looked different—his face was red, hair ruffled beyond repair, sweat pouring off his body and soaking his clothing. Then, in a moment, Spur knew.

He walked Burriss into one of the open cells, pushed him into it, and swung the door shut.

"Put this in the safe," Spur barked, slamming the saddlebag onto the desk.

The boy jumped and followed the man's orders. While he did so Spur walked to the gun rack behind the desk. One of the rifles had been fired recently—he could smell the gunpowder in the barrel.

"You're Gardner's son, right?" Spur asked as the boy dialed the last digit on the safe lock.

"That's right," he said, then pulled the handle to the right. The door opened and he stuffed the bag inside.

"And you were there this morning," Spur said. It was not a question. "You went without your father's permission, then either got scared or trigger-happy and fired the early shot."

The boy stood and stared at Spur in astonishment.

"How did you know?"

"Never mind. Your father doesn't know," Spur said. "Not from what I could tell. Am I right, that you went there without his permission?"

The boy nodded. "He told me I had to stay here. I'm bored sitting here behind this desk all alone, playing solitaire, whittling. So I snuck away this morning and went out there."

"You could have ruined my chance to bring in the killers," Spur said sternly.

"I'm sorry." The boy looked at him blankly, but his cheeks were apple-red.

Spur coughed. "Tell your father when he gets back that I'll be in to see him later."

"Okay," the boy said, still smiling.

"And now you won't be so lonely. You can talk to old Burriss back there." Spur smiled and left the jail. He went to the Calico Hotel, cleaned up, and made it to the kitchen, where he sweet-talked the cook into making him some flapjacks and frying a couple eggs. Spur helped himself to a cup of fresh coffee and sat alone in the dining room, sipping it, trying to drive the chill out of his bones.

He wolfed down the meal as if he hadn't eaten in days, then went outside. Lucas. The Parker case was finished. That left the killing of Fred Lucas.

He could question each farmer in turn, and finally force the guilty party to reveal himself, but that would take a week or more. Farms were scattered all over the county.

Spur sighed and winked at Roxanna as she strolled by, a middle-aged man at her side.

"Spur!" he heard a man call behind him.

Spur turned and saw Gardner limping toward him.

"What's up, Sheriff?"

"Something so important I had to ride all the way back here to tell you about it, and to check. I was right."

"About what?"

"About Fred Lucas. Seems he was wanted for murder in Wyoming two years ago."

CHAPTER TWENTY

"Lucas was wanted for murder?" Spur asked.

Gardner nodded. "I'd gotten a wanted poster on him some time before he moved here, but forgot all about it. I found it in my office in the bottom of a drawer." Gardner produced the poster. It didn't have a picture, but Fred Lucas's name dominated the page.

"Seems he killed a woman in Cheyenne two years ago, trying to rape her. Her husband tracked down the man's name but he'd left town by then. They never caught him."

"And he's been living right here under your nose all these years?" Spur asked.

"I can't believe it myself."

"Why's this so important you had to ride back here from the Craig farm to tell me?"

Gardner smiled. "The name of the woman Fred Lucas killed was Kathryn Lanford."

Lanford. Carl Lanford.

"Lanford killed Lucas," Spur suggested.

"It seems likely. One thing puzzles me. Why didn't Lanford kill him a long time ago? He's been here a year."

"I don't know. I'll ask him."

"You know how to get to the Lanford place?"

"No."

"Ride east for two miles, go north through the corn fields for about a mile, then pick up the trail heading back east again. It's the small farm with a house that has twisted chimneys— two of them."

"Thanks for your help."

"Better late than never," Gardner said, solemnly.

Spur rode through endless rows of short, vibrantly green corn fields. Just when he'd figured he'd ridden a mile the fields abruptly changed; now young wheat struggled up toward the sun. He found the trail and headed toward the east, then rode down it between corn and wheat.

Spur found the house with no difficulty; the chimneys were indeed built of bricks and twisted to make spirals. Smoke rose from one of them. The farm wasn't large, but then again Lanford wasn't a family man, Spur thought grimly as he rode up to it.

Spur tied his horse up before the house and walked toward it.

"What the hell do you want?"

An overweight man dressed in muddy clothing approached him, a shotgun in his hands. Spur smelled boots and stale sweat as the man neared him.

"I'm looking for Lanford."

"Not here." He eyed Spur suspiciously.

McCoy paused. "Where is he?"

"North fields."

"Thanks."

He left the man and rode north. Spur found Lanford on his knees, bent over, a horse standing quietly beside him in the middle of a wheat field.

"Lanford?" Spur asked, then dismounted.

The man looked up in surprise. "Yes?"

"Spur McCoy. Remember me?"

"Who?" Lanford said, then shook his head in confusion.

Spur drew his Colt.

"Wait a minute," Lanford said, rising and dusting off his hands on his pant legs. "What's going on here?"

"Did you kill Fred Lucas?"

Lanford didn't seem surprised by the question. "What makes you say that?"

"As I understand it," Spur said, uneasy at the man's attitude, "Lucas killed your wife."

"That's right. How do you know?"

"Gardner found Lucas on an old wanted poster, saw your wife's name, and figured it out."

"I'll be damned," Lanford said. "I didn't think he had it in him."

"You want to tell me what happened?" Spur asked.

Lanford nodded. "I first met Fred Lucas in Cheyenne about two years ago, a year before I moved to Kearney County. I was there with my wife, Katie. We were visiting relatives—my brother's family, staying in a hotel downtown the night before the trip back east. That night Katie said she had to go out for a walk. She couldn't sleep. The window was stuck and it was a hot night. I said I'd go with her; she said that this was the west and everyone knew that women were safe here. I pulled on my boots but she made it out of the room before me, ran down the stairs and went outside. By the time I got out there she was gone—nowhere in sight." He stopped for a moment. When he continued his voice was tighter. "A few seconds later I heard a scream." Lanford swallowed loudly. "I could always recognize her voice, even when she was screaming. I followed it and found her and Fred Lucas struggling in an alley. He had half-ripped her blouse off, and had one hand between her legs." His face screwed up with emotion as he continued. "I saw a flash of metal between them as I ran toward them. Katie pulled out the derringer she always kept tucked inside her dress in case of trouble while we were travelling. Somehow, he got hold of it and fired, sending a bullet into my sweet Katie. She died before I could reach her." He bent his head back, staring at the sky. "Lucas slugged me and ran. I found out his name but that was it. After a year I stopped looking for him and finally settled here, decided to try my hand at farming."

"When did you realize Lucas lived in the area?" Spur asked.

"Only a few days ago. That day we talked—in the saloon, remember?—I saw Lucas for the first time. He was the one in that stand-off with the farm boy. I finally recognized him."

"So you decided to kill him?"

"That's right. Pay the goddamned bastard back! I knew killing him wouldn't bring back my Katie, but I had to do it."

Spur eased up on his arm.

"Don't move," a greasy voice said from behind him.

McCoy started to turn but a round slammed past him at close range.

"I said it, and I meant it," the man growled. "You all right, Mr. Lanford?"

"I'm fine, Otis."

"What's going on here?" he asked.

"None of your goddamned business!" Spur said.

"You shut your mouth!" Otis said. "Drop that weapon. I want to see it hit the ground. Now!"

"If you kill me I'll kill Lanford," Spur said, his arm directed at the man's chest.

"Shit," Otis said. "What should I do, Mr. Lanford?"

"Do what he says," Lanford's voice sounded tired, lifeless.

"But—" he started.

"You want to get me killed?" Lanford asked.

"He doesn't," Spur said. He spun around and saw the fat man with the dirty clothes standing there. "Throw your rifle down."

217

"Damn. Damn!" he said. "I don't know what to do, Mr. Lanford."

"Otis," Lanford said, as Spur glanced back at him. "Drop the rifle. Now!" he barked.

The man nodded and laid the rifle reverently on the drying mud.

"Now back away," Spur said.

Once Otis had done so, Spur turned to Lanford. "Get up."

Lanford did so. "Otis!" he began. "You stupid son of a bitch!"

"Now stand behind our loyal hand," Spur said.

"Why?"

"You're going to tie him up." Spur tossed Lanford a length of rope from his saddlebag and watched as he did the job. He checked the knots; they were good and sound.

"Otis?" Spur said. "I want you to start walking."

"Walking? Where?"

"That way." Spur pointed toward the north. "Just keep walking until you get out of breath, then turn around and come back. If you try to follow us or bother me again I'll fill you with so many holes you'll breathe through your belly."

"Mr. Lanford!"

"Move!" Spur ordered.

Otis started walking, looking back at them every few steps. The man was slow, Spur thought. He laughed and tied Lanford's hands behind his back, then helped the man into his saddle.

"Where are we going?" Lanford asked.

"Gardner's hotel."

As they rode, Spur behind Lanford's horse, rifle in hands, the agent continued to ask questions.

"Why kill Lucas now?"

"I thought, after the Parkers were killed, if Lucas was murdered everyone would think it was a kind of blacklash for the Parkers. Thought it would throw off suspicion. And one day I just told myself that he had to die—I couldn't take it any more."

"Why didn't yo give the facts to Gardner and let him handle it?"

Lanford laughed. "Where's the satisfaction? That man murdered my wife. If I didn't kill him I'd never be able to rest at night. Seeing him hang wouldn't have done it."

"You know you'll probably hang?"

"Sure," Lanford said.

"You shouldn't have taken the law into your own hands. That's what you pay Gardner for."

"Don't you see?" Lanford said as they bounced along. "I couldn't live until Lucas was dead. Now that he is, I don't care what happens to me. Since Katie's been gone—" he shook his head.

"Maybe the judge will be lenient," Spur said. "I'll give you a good report. You didn't give me any trouble. But that Otis—"

Lanford laughed. "Otis! Hah! He's not too bright, but a damn good watchdog. I hired him on a few weeks ago when the ranchers got busy."

Spur nodded. "Lanford, you neary started an

epidemic. If you hadn't killed Lucas the Craigs probably never would have had the trouble they've seen."

"I know," he said. "I felt responsible for that, in part. But like I told you—now that he's dead, nothing else matters."

They rode the rest of the way in silence, while Spur tried to figure out how to halt the tensions in the area between farmer and rancher.

CHAPTER TWENTY-ONE

AFTER SPUR had deposited Lanford at the jail he headed for the Calico Hotel.

"Ginny?" he said as he walked in. She must have gone out. Spur stripped to the waist, poured fresh water in the basin, washed his face and chest, then shaved. After a night spent crouching in the shadows Spur felt dirty.

Spur splashed the last remnants of shaving soap from his face and toweled dry. As he turned back toward the bed the door opened—and Ginny Burriss walked into the room.

"Oh!" she said in surprise.

"Hello."

She ran to him then, her breasts bouncing gently as she hurried across the floor. They kissed; tongues clashing through lips. He raised his head.

"Ginny," he said.

"Hmmmm?"

"About your father—"

"I know," she said. "I heard all about it."

"I'm sorry."

"Why? The very fact that he's capable of doing such a thing proves he's not the father I used to have. I wanted to break free of him; I guess this is about as free as I can get." She looked at him. "What'll they do to him?" Ginny asked, hesitantly, as if not wishing to hear the answer.

"Don't think about it," Spur said, smiling. "You've got other things to worry about."

"Like what?" she asked. "Do you mean business? Selling the house?"

"No." He pulled her closer and stuck his tongue in her ear. "Like this," he said, between licks.

Ginny shivered. "Sounds wonderful."

"Glad you approve." He kicked the door closed, locked it, then lay her down on the bed.

Ginny squealed as his hands flew over her, unbuttoning, unfastening, pulling off, down and up, gradually denuding her to reveal her magnificent young body—large breasts, slender waist, curving hips.

"Jesus, Ginny!" Spur said. "You've got a beautiful body. And what great tits!" He took one in his mouth.

"Why do I get the idea you like tits?" she asked playfully, running her fingers through the hair matted on his chest.

"Because I'm a tit man. I've always loved them. Can't help myself."

Her hands fumbled at his crotch as she moaned, feeling the hardness straining against the cloth, yanking the cloth away from the buttons. Ginny pushed his pants down below his hips and then slipped his short drawers down.

She gasped as his penis sprang up.

"Spur, you've got the biggest cock I've ever seen!" She gripped his shaft, squeezed it gently, and sent ecstasy through Spur's body.

He jumped up from the bed, pulling out of her hand, and tugged his clothing off, then stood next to the bed, holding himself.

"Put it in me," she said. "Fuck me as hard as you want. Ram it inside me and fill me up." She touched his penis again, making it jerk in response. "I want to be covered by your hairy body. Come here, Spur McCoy." She spread her legs wide and parted her lips.

Spur pounced on her, then knelt between her legs and held them high. He scooted her forward a few inches, laid her feet under his arms, and guided his penis to her slot.

Gradually, painfully slow, Spur pushed into her. Ginny practically screamed out in need, finally pushing herself back against him, driving it into her until her buttocks touched his hairy thighs.

"Oh, yes!" she said, eyes staring dreamily at him. "That's it! You're way up inside me! Oh God, I'm going to come any minute. And I'm going to make you come!"

Spur kissed her, then withdrew and plunged back in. Ginny gasped as he drove down into her, moving her head slightly from side to side.

Ginny just seemed to suck him in, Spur

thought as he continued to pump. Their bodies worked together precisely, hips moving in counterpoise to enhance their lust. Spur savagely thrust into Ginny, attacking her nipples with his mouth; licking, gently biting and sucking.

"Wait, Spur," Ginny said in mid-sigh. "Let's do it standing up."

Spur stopped in mid-stroke. "Really?"

"Yes. Come on; I know it'll be fun. I've—thought about doing it this way." She squirmed beneath him.

Spur rolled to one side and watched as Ginny got to her feet and bent over, her hands on the wall for support, exposing her beautiful hard-as-apples bottom and lips.

He grunted at the sight, feeling his penis spasm. Spur stood and moved close behind her, then pushed easily into her soft wetness. They both sighed at the incredible feeling. Spur gripped the woman's waist as he pumped into her.

She had damn good ideas, Spur thought as he listened to the woman moan and pant. She slammed her buttocks back against him, meeting his strokes, juicy sounds coming from their crotches.

Just as Spur was completely caught up in passion, when his brain kicked off and he was nothing more than an uncontrolled lust-blinded animal, Ginny pulled away from him and stood. Spur nearly yelled when he felt cold air around his shaft.

"One more," she said, pointing to the chair in the corner.

Spur looked at it and shook his head. "Jesus, Ginny! I don't know—how would you do it?"

"Sit down and you'll see!" she smiled at him and stuck a finger up into herself.

He swallowed and slapped down in the chair. Ginny raised herself until she sat on Spur's lap, facing him, her legs straddling the chair's arms. Spur positioned his hands under her bottom and she slowly sank down onto him.

McCoy didn't know how much more of this treatment he could take. She raised off him a second, then plunged down so hard it made her choke. She repeated the motion, and reached behind her to cup his testicles in her hand, pulling gently at them, giving them a yank once in a while, sending shock waves through his nervous system.

Spur kissed her breasts as they bounced before him, then leaned his head back against the wall, his lips parted, sucking in breath as Ginny continued to ride him. The feeling was unbelievable.

"Oh, Spur, I've dreamed of this!" Ginny cried as she impaled herself. "And it's much better than the dreams. I wonder if that's true about all my dreams."

"Dreams?"'

"That's right," she said. "I daydream a lot." She tensed up around him with hidden muscles, nearly sending Spur over the brink.

"That's all," he said. "No more playing

around." He firmly locked Ginny's ankles around his waist, then told her to grab his neck. Spur gently leaned forward and stood, still planted deep inside her. He slowly walked to the bed, bouncing hard into her each step. Spur gently laid her on the mattress then, holding her legs widely spread, pulled out and rammed into her at lightning speed, feeling the sexual tension increase, the pressure grow more intense at his crotch.

Finally he gasped as his pent-up sperm gushed up into her. His body shook, jerked erratically, his hips jamming forward, riding up on her so that she could share his pleasure. Ginny's body moved with his as she sighed through her own pleasure, wrapping her legs more tightly around Spur's torso.

McCoy shot his last and slumped forward, then moved over to lay face up on the bed beside Ginny. Her legs slipped back to the mattress, and she laid a hand on Spur's thigh, then touched the tip of his penis. She trailed out a long, glistening string of his essence.

"Spur," she said.

"What?" His voice was hoarse; he coughed and tried to control his breathing.

"I've—I've decided what to do."

"Just now?"

"Yes. My father's in jail, and he'll hang before long. I know that. There's nothing to keep me here in Kearney. I'll sell as much as I can, have the rest shipped back home to my grandmother —my mother died giving birth to a dead baby— and make some money."

"Money?" Spur asked.

Ginny lifted her eyebrows twice, then fluttered her lashes suggestively.

Spur couldn't conceal a look of surprise. "You're going to do it?"

"These last few minutes," she said. "Weren't they wonderful?"

"Of course."

"Then wouldn't it make sense to do it all the time?"

"Of course; if you can handle it."

"I think I can. That's why I've definitely decided to become a fancy lady." She looked triumphantly into Spur's eyes. "It's the only thing I can do."

"And I helped you make this decision?"

"Yes. If we'd just had a terrible time, I'd probably become a nun, or get married right away—if I could find a man who'd want me. No; this is what I want to be." She smiled. "And if they're all like you—'"

"They won't be," Spur said. "You'll have smelly cowboys, ancient old timers, men who'll want to stick it up your—well, all kinds of men. All shapes, sizes and colors. You ever sleep with a Mexican man?"

"No," she said. "Not yet. But I've dreamed about it. And I don't think badly about a person, just because he may happen to be Mexican, or Indian, or anything! As long as a man has one and knows how to use it, fine! Let's do it!"

"That's good," Spur said. "I hope you're happy with your new career." He kissed her. "Where are you going to go?"

"I don't know. Anywhere off the plains. Maybe San Francisco. I heard they had trees up there; I love trees." She sat up and rubbed her eyes. "So much to do. I really should be going." She bent and kissed his chest. "Thanks for everything you've done for me."

She dressed, Spur helping her by holding up garments until she could slip into them. Completely dressed, she walked to the door and turned back to him.

"For you, Spur, no charge." She winked and was gone.

Spur lay back on the bed; naked, exhausted. He woke when he felt something wet and warm against his penis. A head moved there, long black hair hiding the face. Who was it?

The unseen mouth swallowed his shaft and sucked in earnest, licking, tongueing the sensitive underside.

Spur lifted the head—it rose and the hair fell back from its face revealing Leah Craig smiling at him—with her mouth full.

"Leah," he said.

She pulled off him. "Hi, Spur. I just couldn't let you go without personally thanking you for your help this morning." She lowered her head to the task at hand.

Spur laid back in shock and amazement. He thought he was too tired but Leah's magic soon had him fully stiff again. Spur found his old energy and strength back in force and grabbed Leah's head, holding it still while he pumped into her mouth. After a few seconds of this he relaxed and let her do the work.

Spur's leg dangled off the side of the bed, but he was too awash in pleasure to notice when he began slipping over the side of the bed. Before they realized what had happened they were both on the floor, the sheets between them.

They stood, laughing, and Leah undressed.

"I knew you wouldn't mind if I came right in," she said, "since the door was open. And when I saw you laying there naked, I couldn't help myself."

"Sounds reasonable to me."

Leah stripped off the man's work shirt, the heavy pants, and boots to reveal her perfect body. She lay on the bed next to him and pulled Spur to her. Lying on their sides they plastered their bodies together. Spur cupped her breasts in one hand as they kissed, his eager erection throbbing between them.

She slipped down, lowered her head to his crotch, and greedily enmouthed him again. Spur shivered. He moved with her until he sat on the edge of the bed while Leah knelt before him.

Spur's balls slapped against her chin as she swallowed him, snapping the fuse inside his groin. He pushed down into her throat as he spurted, gripping her head, ramming deep six more times before gently releasing her.

Spur laid her back on the bed, exhausted, gazing at the ceiling as Leah sucked the last from him, blessing the day he'd first come to Kearney County.

CHAPTER TWENTY-TWO

As Spur walked into Gardner's office he saw a woman standing, her back to him, talking to the sheriff.

"I certainly don't blame you," she said.

Spur recognized the voice before she turned around—Amanda Tate.

"Mrs. Tate," Spur said, tipping his hat and setting down his bag.

"Mr. McCoy." She smiled slightly and approached him. "I'm glad I have this chance to see you before you leave."

"We were just talking about Roscoe," Gardner said, standing on the opposite side of his desk.

"I'm sorry, Mrs. Tate."

"No need." She stiffened her back. "He was a bad apple, that's for sure, and it wasn't your fault that he murdered the Parkers, or attacked the Craig farm. You did what you had to do. That's in the past now."

"How's Mr. Craig feeling?"

"My husband?" She smiled. "It's the strangest thing; he woke up this morning feeling much better. He even took a walk around his room. I can't say why, but it looks like he's on the road to recovery."

"Glad to hear that," Spur said.

"Well," she said, pushing her hands back into the gloves she held, "I should be getting back home. I hear Wesley outside yelling to me." She put out her hand for Spur to take. "Thank you again for all your help."

"My pleasure." He kissed the gloved hand and released it.

"Goodbye, Spur." With a smile to the sheriff she left.

"A fine woman, Amanda is," Gardner said after a few seconds. "Too bad she had such a piss-poor son as Roscoe."

"That's not her fault," Spur said. "Everything finished up here?"

Gardner nodded. He motioned toward Burriss's cell. The man sat in the corner, eyes downcast.

"He's been quiet—not a work from him all day."

"He's got a lot to think about."

"I'll say. You leaving us?"

"Yes. I wired back to my office that this job was completed. Within two hours I received a reply. My next assignment."

"Fine," Gardner said.

"There's no problem here, is there?" Spur

asked. "If you think I should stay around for a few days, I could probably do it."

"No need, McCoy. I can handle things from here on in."

"Think there'll be any more trouble?"

"No. I won't tolerate it. I've been too easy. Hell, you never would have had to come here in the first place if I'd gotten off my butt and worked with my suspicions! You've shown me that can be the solution. I'll also admit I was afraid of the situation."

"Afraid?"

"I worried it would end up worse if I messed with it. But from now on in—I'm in charge."

"Glad to hear it," Spur said. "If you ever need me—you know where to reach me."

"St. Louis?" Gardner asked.

"Right. I'm never in my office, but they relay any important messages to me wherever I am."

"Thanks again. I don't know what I would have done without you."

Spur smiled and walked to the door.

"Take care of yourself!" Gardner said.

Spur left the office and walked toward the train station.

"Yoo-hoo!" a high voice said.

Spur looked to his right and saw Roxanna Stafford walking to him, dressed in a spectacular pure white satin creation with cascades of ruffles.

"Hello, Roxanna," Spur said.

"Going somewhere?"

"Headed to the train station. I'm late."

"The station?" Roxanna was shocked. "You're not leaving Kearney, are you?"

"Yes."

"But—but—hell, Spur McCoy!" she said, exasperated. "You led me on all this time, saying you owed me, and now I catch you trying to sneak out of Kearney without even saying goodbye! Don't I deserve something for all the help I gave you?"

"I was going to stop by and see you, but I'm behind schedule." He meant it.

"You're seeing me now," Roxanna swung her hips back and forth lewdly. Two cowboys riding by whooped, and Roxanna turned to blow them kisses.

"I have to catch the five-ten," Spur said. "Otherwise, I'd have to wait another day. I can't afford to do that."

"Come on, Spur—one for the road. It won't take long. Hell, I'll even do it here." She put her hand to her dress and pulled down its front, revealing more of her splendid breasts. "Look good, don't they?"

Spur debated a moment—if they hurried—

No. He didn't have the time. Besides, Leah and Ginny had already wrung him dry. He doubted he could do it again so soon.

"Sorry, Roxanna. Not this time."

She sighed. "I don't like a man who turns me down," she said, "but I'll live. Next time you're passing through look me up, or lick me up!" Roxanna laughed.

"I'll do that."

"Hey, I heard you caught Roscoe, Jack and Rev. Burriss all with their hands dirty," she said, snickering. "That's what you were doing all this time in Kearney, right? That's why you asked me all those questions, listened in on Roscoe and me in the closet. Right?"

"Yes."

"Heard you were some government man, working for the Secret Service. You heading on to your next job?"

"That's right."

"Well—hell," she said, then lunged at him. She threw her arms around him and pressed her mouth to his.

Spur recovered from his surprise and returned her kiss, their tongues lashing each other. Spur heard an old woman shriek at the sight of such unbridled passion on the street in broad daylight.

"Whew!" Roxanna said. "That was sweet. Take care of it," she said, still pushed up against him. "I wouldn't want anything to happen to it before I got a change to play."

"I'll try."

She smiled and walked away.

Spur set down his carpetbag on the floor of the Kearney train station, thinking of the people he'd met in the past few days. Suddenly a hand tapped his shoulder.

Spur spun around. Ginny Burriss stood before him, dressed for travel, holding two bags.

"Going my way?" she asked.

Spur smiled and kissed her, then took her bags and lifted his own as the train puffed up.

"You finished your business here?" Spur asked as the sound died down.

Ginny nodded. "One man's wanted the house for years, and he bought it on the spot. Paid cash. With that money and what I'll get from my father I'm pretty well set. So I've decided to go on an expedition to see what I can find in the real world out there. I wouldn't mind sharing part of it with you," she said invitingly.

Spur smiled. They climbed the steps and entered the train.

Perhaps it wouldn't be so boring a ride after all.